A Soft Place to Land

Soft A Place to Land

JANAE MARKS

KATHERINE TEGEN BOOKS
An Imprint of HarperCollins Publishers

Katherine Tegen Books is an imprint of HarperCollins Publishers.

A Soft Place to Land
Text copyright © 2021 by Janae Marks
Interior art © 2021 by Ronique Ellis

Library of Congress Cataloging-in-Publication Data
Names: Marks, Janae, author.
Title: A soft place to land / Janae Marks.
Description: First edition. | New York : Katherine Tegen Books, an
imprint of HarperCollins Publishers 2021. | Audience: Ages 8–12. |
Audience: Grades 4–6. | Summary: Twelve-year old Joy dreams of
writing music for the movies, but first she has to survive her
family's move into a small apartment when her father loses his job.
Identifiers: LCCN 2021016334 | ISBN 978-0-06-287587-7 (hardcover)
Subjects: CYAC: Apartment houses—Fiction. | Family life—Fiction. |
Friendship—Fiction. | Moving, Household—Fiction. | African
Americans—Fiction.
Classification: LCC PZ7.1.M3722 So 2021 | DDC 813.6 [Fic]—dc23
LC record available at https://lccn.loc.gov/2021016334

Typography by Laura Mock
21 22 23 24 25   PC/LSCH   10 9 8 7 6 5 4 3 2 1
❖
First Edition

For Steve
Home is wherever I'm with you

Chapter One

I may only be twelve, but I've already fallen in love once—with music. With film scores, to be exact.

The moment it happened, when I first realized how magical movie scores can be, was around Christmas last year. Mom got two tickets through work for *Star Wars: The Empire Strikes Back* in concert. She invited me to come with her. The New York Philharmonic orchestra performed the soundtrack live on stage, while the movie played on a huge screen above them.

It was already a special night because Mom and I drove into Manhattan together. I got to wear my favorite dress, which is made from the softest velvet the color of cranberries. On the car ride down, we sang along to the radio. Mom also asked me about school and my friends, and it was so nice to talk to her—just the two of us, without my little sister interrupting with her own questions and comments. Before heading to the theater, we got dinner at a fancy soul food restaurant where I had the best cornbread I've ever tasted.

The concert itself was incredible. I'd seen all the *Star Wars* movies before, but this time, the music swirled around the theater, bouncing off the walls, giving me goose bumps. The scenes were even more dramatic with the orchestra playing right in front of us. The story came alive in a whole new way.

I came alive in a whole new way. By the time we walked out of the theater, I felt like a different Joy.

On the drive home, I downloaded the main theme song from the movie and made it my phone's ringtone. Then I stared at the concert program, at the names and pictures of the people who'd created the music. The composer's name was John Williams, and his bio said he composed the score for nine *Star Wars* movies. I decided right then and there that I wanted to do that, too.

I'm going to compose music for movies. I'm going to make other people feel the way that I did that night at the concert. One day, people are going to fill a theater to hear an orchestra play my music.

I have it all figured out. I love a good plan. And a list. Step one is to learn how to play the piano.

But before I can get to that, I have to survive this move.

"Can I go for a walk?" I ask Mom. "I want to check out the park behind the building."

Mom's holding a box cutter and leaning over one of the billion boxes piled up around the apartment. They look like the blocks my six-year-old sister, Malia, used to play with. She'd stack them up to make the highest tower, carefully adding blocks one by one. Then she'd count to three and knock it all down. The bigger the mess, the wider she'd grin. And then she'd start all over again.

"Please?" I add. "I'm getting claustrophobic in here."

"What about me? I want to go to the playground," Malia whines from her spot on the couch. She's huddled in the only corner that's not covered with black garbage bags practically exploding with things we brought from our house. Her tablet is on her lap.

I give Mom a look that says, *Please let me go alone.* I had to babysit Malia for the last couple of hours while my parents moved all of our stuff in here, and I'm ready for some time by myself. Especially since Malia and I have to share a bedroom from now on. I can hear Dad in our room digging through his tool bag and moving parts around as he gets ready to put together our new bunk bed.

"I'll take you to the playground before dinner, okay?" Mom tells Malia. To me, she says, "Sure, have fun."

"Bring water," she adds. "It's hot out there. Thank goodness this place came with air conditioning."

I go into our new apartment's tiny kitchen to fill my reusable water bottle. My mom calls it a galley kitchen because it's a narrow room with the cabinets and appliances on either side. It can barely fit all four of us at once. The kitchen in our house was at least three times bigger.

Once my bottle is full, I put my headphones on, turn on my playlist of favorite movie scores, and go out into the hallway. I pause to take a deep breath with my eyes closed, and I try to channel the way I felt the night of the philharmonic concert. At least I still have music. Nobody can take that away from me. Maybe it'll help me get through this.

I press the elevator button and try to guess which of the two elevators will arrive first. I pick the one on the right, but then the left elevator door opens. There's a girl standing inside it, leaning against the back wall. I think I recognize her from my new middle school, which I transferred to last week. I'm pretty sure she's in my grade. We aren't in any of the same classes, so I don't know her name yet. I smile politely as I move to stand next to her.

The girl taps my shoulder. I pull my headphones down and turn toward her.

"Hi!" she says, sounding way too cheerful. "I'm Nora. Apartment 5B. Did you just move in?"

"Yeah. Hi. I'm Joy. Uh, apartment . . . 3C." Is that how people introduce themselves around here, by their apartment numbers?

"You're the new kid at school, right?" she asks.

I nod. "Not new to town, though. I used to go to the other middle school."

"Cool. What were you listening to?" Nora asks.

"Huh?"

She points to the headphones around my neck. "Were you listening to music?"

"Oh. Um, yeah. Songs from movie soundtracks. The *Jurassic Park* theme song was playing," I say.

The elevator stops at the lobby floor, and we both get off. I'm about to say goodbye and walk away when Nora starts talking again.

"*Wait.* Are you into movies, too?" Before I can answer, Nora keeps talking. "I'm super into them. I want to become a filmmaker when I grow up. I'm working on a screenplay right now. It's almost done. Then I'm going to start filming. But before I do that, I want to save up for a better camera, and also some editing software. When I send my movie to film festivals, I want people to be surprised when they find out a kid made it."

Nora practically says that entire thing with one breath. That's how fast she speaks.

"Wow. Good luck," I say. "That's . . . really cool. I'm obsessed with movie scores. The music. I actually want to compose my own someday."

Nora's eyes widen with excitement. "Seriously? Oh my gosh, I can't believe we're both into movies! Maybe you can help me with the music in mine when I'm done filming."

"Yeah, maybe. What's your movie about?"

"It's about a mom and daughter who go on a road trip together, but then all sorts of things go wrong."

"That sounds fun," I say. "How'd you come up with the idea?"

"It's inspired by my mom, Nadia Ramos. She died when I was six." She says it so matter-of-factly.

My mouth opens in surprise, and I immediately regret using the word "fun."

"Colon cancer," Nora adds.

"I am *so* sorry," I say.

"It's okay. I miss her of course. But I've still got my little sister, Izzy, plus my dad. And he's the best."

I smile but still feel awkward.

Nora is opening up about something so . . . personal . . . so easily. To a stranger. But something about her honesty makes me want to tell her something honest about myself, too.

"Well," I start. "My family and I moved here because we had to sell our house. My dad lost his job a few months ago, and they couldn't afford the mortgage anymore. It was going to"—I pause to remember the word my parents used—"foreclose, and the bank was going to take it away from us. But before that happened, my parents put it up for sale and found a new family to buy it." I swallow, and there's a big lump in my throat. I lived in that house for my entire life until today. It felt like a member of my family, that now we've lost. Saying goodbye to it this morning was the hardest thing I've ever had to do.

I blink a bunch of times so I won't cry.

Mom and Dad told me that foreclosures happen to a lot of families. But it hasn't happened to anyone else I know.

They also said that it's lucky our house sold so fast, and we found an affordable apartment in our same town. Things could be a lot worse.

I find that hard to imagine.

"I know it's nothing like losing a parent," I add, "but I'm still sad about it. I love that house. I had so many happy memories there. Now some other family gets to make memories there. And I have to share a room with my little sister now. I love her, but she's half my age. I liked having my own space. It stinks."

Nora stares at me, like she's really listening, and I regret saying so much. I just met this girl. What if Nora's reaction makes me feel worse about everything?

Before I can turn and run away, Nora responds with, "I get it. I hate change, too."

I exhale, relieved.

"But this building is actually pretty great," Nora adds. "I mean, everyone's so nice. And I love having the park right behind us. Have you been over there yet?"

"I'm actually going to walk over there now." I swallow. "Do you . . . want to come with me?"

"I'd love to!" she says, and I grin. "But I can't. I told my dad that I'd finish my laundry. Another time?" Nora asks.

"Sure," I say, disappointed.

"I get what you mean about sharing a room with your sister," Nora says. "My sister and I share, too. She's nine, and she definitely annoys me sometimes, but we make the most of it. If things get tense or whatever, have a dance party. Trust me, it fixes almost everything."

I laugh. "Okay."

"But if you need a place to escape, let me know. I know the perfect spot," Nora adds.

"Really?"

"Yeah." She lowers her voice and gives me a sly smile. "But it's top secret."

Chapter Two

A top secret place? I don't get to hear more about it because Nora's phone alarm sounds and she has to grab her laundry. But I can't stop thinking about it for the rest of the day. Next time I see her, I need to find out what place she was talking about. Because it's only day one in this apartment, and I'm more than ready to escape already.

"Guess what?" Malia asks that night as we get ready for bed. "Mom says she's gonna buy us new comforters so they match. Curtains too. We get to help pick them out."

"Nice," I say. Right now nothing in here matches,

since our old rooms had completely different styles. At least it's almost all unpacked, since it's where my parents spent most of their time today.

I pull a pair of pajama shorts and a T-shirt out of my drawer in the pink dresser from Malia's old room. I sit on the yellow armchair from my old room while I put them on. I remember when my mom helped me pick out this chair. She said it would add a nice pop of color to my room. Now, surrounded by all of Malia's bright pink stuff, it barely stands out.

Once Malia's dressed for bed, she crawls into the bottom bunk. When I look over, she's hugging her stuffed narwhal, looking all of a sudden like a deflated balloon.

"You miss it, too?" I ask Malia. "The house?"

She nods. "I miss my room. And my old bed. And the backyard. Joy, who's gonna feed the hummingbirds?"

She sticks her lower lip out, a sign that she's about to cry. I have to stop her, right now, or else I'll start crying, too.

I remember Nora's advice from earlier. *Dance party.* I open the music app on my laptop and click on a playlist with songs from Disney movies. The familiar intro from *Frozen*'s "Let it Go" begins.

Malia perks up. "My favorite song!"

"Let's dance." I pull Malia off her bed and we spin

around, wave our arms, and belt out along with the song. I focus on the music and let all thoughts about our house disappear. We're having so much fun that at first, I don't hear Dad knocking on our door frame.

"Malia, time to brush your teeth," he says. "And, Joy, can you turn the music down?"

"Why?" I ask while Malia goes across the hall to the apartment's only bathroom. I used to blast music all the time at our house, and Dad never said anything to me then.

"Because we don't want to disturb the neighbors," Dad says.

"What do you mean?" I ask.

"We're in an apartment building now, so we can't make too much noise."

"It's not noise," I protest. "It's music." The next song that comes on is the orchestra arrangement of Beauty and the Beast, and it's mainly piano and strings.

Dad rubs his chin, which he hasn't shaved in a while since he's growing in a beard. "I know. Just keep it at a lower volume at night, okay? You can still listen to it."

I go over to my laptop and turn down the volume.

"Thanks." Dad lingers and looks around. "Are you happy with your new room?"

Mom appears behind him in the doorway. She's fresh

out of the shower and wearing her blue fuzzy bathrobe. "The bunk beds look great," she says. "When I was a kid, I always wanted one."

Mom's only saying that to make me feel better. "It's fine," I say. I couldn't care less about having a bunk bed. What I want is my old room back. It was perfect—my own private oasis. This room only feels like a place to sleep. But there's one consolation. I point to the empty space next to the closet door. "But look, there's still room over there to squeeze in a piano, especially if we move the bunk beds over a couple inches."

My parents exchange a glance.

"What?" I ask.

Mom looks like she isn't sure if she should say something.

"What is it?" I repeat.

Mom exhales. "Your dad and I talked about the piano, and . . . well . . . we're not going to be able to buy one for you right now."

My stomach drops all the way down to my toes. "*What?*"

"I'm sorry, Joy," Dad says. "We have to be careful with our spending right now."

"But you just sold our house. Don't you have some extra money from that?"

"We owed the bank money," Dad says, his face twisting in discomfort. "So no, we don't."

I look at Mom. "You told Malia you'd buy us new comforters and curtains. Forget about all that and buy the piano instead. I don't need new stuff for our room. I only need a piano."

"The piano is much more expensive than those other things," Mom says.

"But you promised!" I say.

"I know, and we wanted to be able to buy it for you." She sighs heavily, and then says, "There's something else."

Oh no. What other bad news are they going to share?

"We're going to have to stop your piano lessons," she says. "Only for a while."

"No!" I shake my head in disbelief. "You can't!"

"Believe me, we wouldn't if we didn't have to," Dad says. "We have to cut back on all unnecessary spending for a while."

And my piano lessons are unnecessary? This is my dream they're talking about.

"For how long?" I ask. "When can I take lessons again?"

"Hopefully next school year," Mom says. "But I don't know for sure. We were thinking maybe you could switch to another instrument at school, like the violin or clarinet. Then you could join orchestra or band, and they'll lend you an instrument that you can learn to play at school."

"But I don't want to play those instruments. I want to play the piano. You know that." I pause and then ask, "What about Malia's ballet classes? Does she have to quit those, too?"

"What did you say?" Malia asks, coming back from the bathroom. "I have to quit *ballet?*" Her voice goes up an octave, and she looks like she's about to cry again.

"No, sweetie." Mom hugs Malia to her side. "You can still take ballet."

"How?" I ask. "You can pay for ballet but not piano?"

"We paid for the entire year of ballet classes back in the fall," Mom explains.

I shake my head. I'm glad Malia can keep doing ballet, but I wish I could still take piano lessons. I want to become a composer, and all composers know how to play the piano. How can I learn it without a teacher or an instrument to practice on?

"We're really sorry, Joy," Dad says. "This won't be forever."

I nod like I understand, but I don't believe him. We

had to sell our house and move into a random apartment where the walls are too thin and there aren't enough rooms. We aren't going to live in our real home ever again, so how am I supposed to believe that anything will ever be the same?

Chapter Three

As I try to get comfortable on the top bunk, I finally get why Dad warned me about turning the music down. The walls in this building aren't as thick as the ones in our house. Even though our bedroom door is closed, there are all sorts of unfamiliar sounds. Right above me, the floorboard creaks as someone walks across the room. From out in the hallway, there's a screeching noise, followed by a bang—what sounds like somebody opening and closing their apartment door. Then there's the ding of the elevator, and voices as whoever it is gets off and walks down the hall.

There are also sounds coming from outside. This street

is much busier than our old one, so I hear not only the whoosh of cars driving past, but every once in a while, motorcycle drivers revving their engines. It sounds like they're racing down our street.

It's like when my family stays in a hotel when we're on vacation. It's always hard for me to fall asleep in new places, because all the strange noises are distracting, making me feel uneasy. But this time, I won't be checking out of here at the end of a trip.

What if I *never* get used to it?

The worst part of all, though, is that I can hear my parents arguing in their bedroom next to ours. They aren't yelling, but their voices are loud enough for me to make out some of what they're saying.

"I saw you give Spencer cash earlier," Mom says. "What was that for?"

She's talking about Uncle Spencer, my dad's brother, who helped us move today.

"He's borrowing it," Dad says. "He's going to pay me back in a couple of weeks. Before our next rent check is due."

"I'll believe it when I see it." Mom's voice has an edge to it.

This isn't the first time I've heard them argue. Ever since we had to put our house up for sale, they've been fighting more and more. But at the house, my bedroom was at the opposite end of the hallway from theirs. At night, I couldn't hear them at all. Now, there's no way to escape it.

Another motorcycle revs by outside, so I miss some of what Mom and Dad say next.

"I'm thinking of working with him," Dad says, once I can hear them again. "His construction business. I could invest, become his partner."

"Are you serious?" Mom asks.

"Keep your voice down," Dad says.

I hear their bedroom door close, but the walls are thin.

"I'd be doing it for us," Dad says.

At the house, I figured my parents were fighting because the move was stressing them out. But now we're here, and they're still fighting. Is this how it's going to be from now on?

"You know," Mom says. "We'd have some extra money if you took the hardware store job. You can still job search while you work there. Lisa's been telling me that Jeff can use the extra help."

"I already told you I'm not working in a hardware store," Dad says. "I have a master's degree. I'm too qual-ified to work at a register. And for what, seven bucks an hour?"

"Baby, you're too broke not to," Mom says. "Seven bucks an hour is more than you're making now."

Broke. The word echoes around my brain.

For a moment, neither of them say anything else. But then Mom says, "I don't know how much longer I can . . ." Her voice gets quieter, so I don't hear the rest of her sentence.

Mom doesn't know how much longer she can *what*? I wish I knew, because now I'm thinking the worst.

What if my parents split up?

As soon as the thought appears, it's like someone hurled a huge rock at me and knocked me over. I've already lost my home. I can't lose either of my parents.

I can't take it. The fighting. All the strange sounds in this building. This whole apartment. This unfamiliar bedroom. Even this bunk bed. I'm too close to the ceiling, and it's not natural.

All I want to do is go to sleep.

No. What I want is to go back to my real home.

I wish I were back in my old room, in my old bed.

But I can't go back to my house. This is supposed to be home now. And there's nothing that I can do about it.

I hate that so much is out of my control. My parents keep making all of these decisions without talking to me, like my opinion doesn't matter. Dad can lend Uncle

Spencer money, but I can't get a piano or take lessons anymore. I wish I had my own money, so I didn't have to rely on them.

I really wanted that piano.

Before I can stop them, tears spill out of my eyes, wetting my pillowcase. I bury my face in the fabric so Malia won't hear me and wake up. I cry harder than I have since finding out about the move. Then, sniffling, I carefully climb down the bunk bed ladder and look for a tissue, before remembering that we haven't unpacked all of those supplies yet. I don't want to go into the bathroom for toilet paper and risk my parents seeing me. Then they might know that I heard them argue. So instead, I wipe my face on my T-shirt and grab my headphones from my desk. I plug the cord into my phone, slip them over my ears, and turn on the film score from the Disney movie *Up*. It's one of my favorites, and it's the perfect soundtrack to cry to, since the piano music is so soft and beautiful.

As I'm climbing back to the top bunk, I miss a step and lose my balance for a second. I don't fall, but my phone does, hitting the side of the bunk bed before landing on the floor.

Shoot.

Malia shifts in her bed, and I freeze in place, hoping the noise wasn't loud enough to wake her. But in the light of the streetlamp coming from the window, I see Malia open her eyes and rub them.

"What's going on?" she asks in a sleepy voice.

"Nothing." I'm glad it's dark in here so she can't see my puffy eyes. "Go back to sleep." I pick my phone up from the floor and climb back up to the top bunk.

"Are Mommy and Daddy fighting?" Malia asks.

Ugh. I hoped she wouldn't hear that.

"They're just talking," I say, like it's no big deal. "It's fine. Close your eyes."

A few seconds pass, and then Malia says, "Joy?"

"Yes?"

"Can I sleep next to you? Please?"

I sigh. "Sure. I'll come down there."

I carefully climb back down the ladder and crawl into bed with Malia. We huddle together under the covers. She's wearing a silk bonnet like me, and it smells like the shea butter cream Mom puts in her hair before she twists it.

"Now go to sleep," I say.

"Okay," Malia mumbles, sounding even more drowsy. I listen as her breathing slows down and she starts snoring ever so slightly.

For the first time all day, I'm glad to be sharing a room with Malia. I'm glad I'm not alone right now.

I put my headphones back on and turn the music loud enough to drown out every other sound, so I can finally fall asleep.

But sleep still won't come. Partly because I'm squished on this twin mattress with Malia, who's breathing on my neck.

Mostly because I can't stop thinking about everything that happened today—saying goodbye to my house, moving here, meeting Nora.

Actually, meeting Nora was nice. Especially the part where she talked about a place to escape.

What place could she be talking about?

Chapter Four

I want to stop by Nora's apartment to talk to her on Sunday, but I've already forgotten what number it is. I'll have to talk to her at school.

My parents spend all of Sunday unpacking, and the towers of boxes around the apartment begin to disappear. By Monday, when I wake up for school, it really hits me that we live somewhere else now. This isn't some temporary dream that I'm going to wake up from.

I miss my old school and my friends there. I miss getting a strawberry yogurt smoothie from the fridge, putting my headphones on, and walking the ten minutes to school every morning. The walk was always so nice, even in the winter.

One time it had snowed all night, but it stopped early enough for school to still open. I bundled up in all of my winter gear and put on the theme song from *Game of Thrones*. I don't even watch the show, but the music is incredible.

I trudged through the still unshoveled sidewalks with the song energizing my every step. By the time I got to school, the music swelled in my headphones, and it was like I'd reached the top of a mountain.

Now I have to take the bus.

And Dad has to drive Mom to the train station every morning, since they got rid of one of our cars to save more money. They're leaving as I'm brushing my teeth.

Mom comes into the bathroom and kisses my forehead. "Have a good day at school. I have to work late tonight so I won't be home for dinner, but I'll see you later."

"Okay. Bye," I say, with my mouth full of toothpaste foam.

"I'll be right back," Dad says from the bathroom doorway. The apartment and car keys jingle in his hand. "The station is only eight minutes away. When I get back, I'll drop Malia off at school."

Malia's lucky. Her elementary school is a magnet school, so even though we moved across town, she can still keep going there.

I'm staring at the empty fridge when Dad gets back. "I'm making a trip to the store this morning," he says when he finds me in the kitchen. "Here—I grabbed you and Malia blueberry muffins at the train station—the ones you like. And I have lunch money for you. I promise tomorrow things will be more normal."

Normal. I wish that were true.

"Okay." I close the refrigerator door.

Dad is helping Malia look for a sparkly rainbow headband that she insists on wearing when I say goodbye. The bus stop is only two blocks away, but my nerves multiply with every step. I've never had to take the bus to school before. What if nobody wants me to sit next to them? What if the only free seat is up in the front next to the bus driver? Also, sometimes I get motion sick in cars. What if I throw up? Panic rolls through me as I imagine throwing up in front of a busload of kids.

When I get close to the bus stop, I notice three different groups of kids. Some older teenagers stand together, and then a few feet away are kids my age. The last group is elementary school kids wearing backpacks that look

26

huge on their backs. One of them looks like a younger Nora, so I bet it's her little sister.

I spot Nora immediately. She has a Mets baseball hat on, with a ponytail looped through the back. My nerves turn into excitement, since at least now I can finally ask her about the secret place. But what if the other kids at the bus stop don't know about it? Guess I'll have to figure out another time to ask Nora, in private.

None of the kids my age notice me when I walk up to them. They're all looking at someone's phone. The girl holding it is wearing a colorful crown made with real blue and white flowers, with matching ribbons tied at the back, trailing down her long, wavy hair.

I feel weird joining their circle without being invited in. So for a minute, I stand a foot away, watching them. But then I realize how weird it is to stare at them, so I force myself to inch closer and closer until I'm standing right next to Nora.

"Hey." I clear my throat. "What are you all, um, looking at?" Already it's like I'm interrupting something, like I don't belong here.

But then Nora turns around and smiles at me. "Joy, hey!"

I exhale in relief as she moves over, giving me space

to officially join the circle.

"We're looking at pictures of Elena from this weekend," Nora says. "She went to a Renaissance Faire upstate. Isn't her crown gorgeous? She got to wear this whole costume. See?" Nora moves to the side so I can see Elena's phone. In the picture on the screen, Elena's wearing a blue-green fairy costume. It's so elaborate, and her face was painted to match. She wore shimmering wings, and the same flower crown that she's wearing now.

"Wow, you look really pretty," I say.

"Thanks." Elena beams. "I had the best time."

"Joy just moved into our building," Nora says. "3C."

How does she remember that?

"That's next to Miss Mae, right?" asks one of the other kids—a Black boy with a lightning bolt design shaved onto his fade haircut. "Did you meet Ziggy yet?"

"Ziggy? No. Who's that?" I ask.

"Miss Mae's dog. I see him outside or in the elevator sometimes when she takes him out. He's the nicest dog." He pauses. "I'm Miles, by the way."

"I'm Oliver," the other boy says as he gives a shy wave. He has blond hair, green eyes, and is wearing a Webster Middle School Track T-shirt.

"Do all of you go to Webster?" I ask.

"Not me and Miles," Elena says. "But our bus picks us up from here, too."

"They all live in our building, though," Nora says. "So we hang out sometimes."

"Nice," I say.

"Elena's trying to get us to LARP with her," Oliver says.

"To *what?*" I ask.

"LARP. It stands for live-action role-playing," Elena explains. "It's the best thing ever. You get to run around and pretend to be characters, like it's a play. But you're improvising a lot, too. I mostly do it during the summer, at camp. But I was saying it'd be fun if we got our own group together during the school year."

"Sounds . . . interesting," I say.

"It's okay if you're not into it," Nora says. "Elena already knows I'm better behind a camera."

"What kind of stuff *are* you into?" Elena asks me.

"Um, well, I like music," I say. "Movie scores."

"Do they have *Star Wars* LARPs?" Miles interrupts. "Like with lightsabers? Now *that* I would do."

"You're into *Star Wars?*" I ask Miles.

He gives a look of fake shock. "Of course! I've seen all of the movies in the theater with my dad. I mean, except for the ones that came out before I was born."

"I've seen all of them, too," I say. "I'm also obsessed with the music from the movies."

"Which movie is your favorite? Mine is *The Empire Strikes Back*."

"I got to see that one on a big screen!" I say. "With the New York Philharmonic playing the score live."

"For real?" Miles asks.

I smile and nod. "I also really like *The Force Awakens*, because of Rey."

He points at me and says, "Yes. I approve."

Right then, a yellow school bus pulls up to the stop and opens its doors.

"This is ours," Nora tells me. To Elena and Miles, she says, "See you later!"

They wave as Oliver, Nora, and I file onto the bus. It's about half full.

Nora sits in a seat in the middle of the bus, and Oliver sits across from her. He takes out a sketchbook and pen and starts doodling.

"He does that every day," she tells me. "Now I have you to talk to!"

I take that as an invitation to sit next to her.

"Have you made any friends at school yet?" Nora asks.

"Not really," I admit. "But I only started last week."

I miss my friends from my old school, the ones who

promised to keep in touch after I moved. But I haven't heard from them once.

"A lot of my friends are from the broadcasting club," Nora says.

"What's that?" I ask.

"It's the club that produces the weekly news show that airs on Friday mornings on our classroom TVs. Anyway, you should come sit at our table during lunch."

I smile. "Okay."

Nora and I talk about our favorite movies and soundtracks, and start listing movies to watch together sometime. I write the list down in the Notes app of my phone, and place movie reel emojis at the top. I have a bunch of other lists in the app already—favorite movie scores, songs I want to learn to play on the piano, things I'll miss about my old house that I don't want to forget.

The next thing I know, the bus is pulling up in front of school. I didn't even throw up!

We walk off the bus, and when Nora, Oliver, and I get inside school, we wave goodbye to each other.

"See you at lunch?" Nora asks.

I nod, grateful to have made a few new friends.

Chapter Five

After school, I'm on the couch reading a book for homework when the doorbell rings. When I open the front door, a small tan dog sprints into the apartment and down the hallway, like it knows exactly where it's going.

I stand there, momentarily frozen.

"Ziggy!" the older woman standing at the door yells after the dog. To me she says, "I'm so sorry. Ziggy knew the previous tenants. There was a little boy, and Ziggy seems to think he still lives here."

Oh, Ziggy, I think. *The dog Miles was talking about. This must be Miss Mae.* "That's okay," I say, still not sure what to do next. Should I go get the dog from wherever he ran?

Should I let her inside to get him?

"Ziggy!" she shouts again, and a few seconds later, the dog marches back into the living room.

Malia runs in behind him, grinning. "Oh my gosh, Joy! Did you see this puppy? Where did he come from? Is he ours?" Once she sees the woman at the door, Malia gets quiet and stands next to me.

I lean down to get a better look at Ziggy. He's a French bulldog. He actually looks a little disappointed, and I feel bad for him. He must've really loved that little boy. I reach down and scratch him behind his ears, and he licks my hand as a thank-you.

Once Malia sees that, she tentatively pets Ziggy, too, and she giggles when he licks her back.

"I'm Mae Willoughby," the woman says. "But you can call me Mae. I live right next to you, and wanted to come over and say hello."

"I'm Joy, and this is Malia. My mom's still at work, and my dad is downstairs in the laundry room. He'll be back in a minute. Do you, um, want to come in?" I know I'm not supposed to talk to strangers, but this lady and her dog don't seem very dangerous.

"Sure, as long as you don't mind Ziggy."

"I don't mind." I pet him again. He jumps up on my knee and starts kissing my face.

"He's so cute," Malia squeals. "Look at his wrinkly face."

"He seems to like you two," Mae says with a smile.

"Sorry this place is a mess." I tilt my head toward the boxes in the corner of our living room. "My parents are still unpacking. But you can sit down on the couch if you want."

"Thank you." Before she goes to sit, Mae hands over a Tupperware container. "Here, I brought you something."

I crack open the top, and between sheets of wax paper are cookies. I inhale the cinnamon and sugar.

"Wow, they smell amazing. Thanks," I say.

"You're welcome. Snickerdoodles are my signature cookie. I like to bake them with my grandkids."

I remove two cookies, giving one to Malia.

Her whole face lights up. "Best. Day. Ever," she whispers.

I take a bite of my cookie, and it's perfectly chewy. "This is so yummy," I say, and Mae grins. I put the Tupperware down on our dining room table.

As I finish chewing, the front door opens and Dad walks in, carrying an empty laundry basket. Ziggy runs up to him and starts jumping up his leg.

"Ziggy!" Mae says firmly. "Get down."

"Oh. Hello," Dad says with a laugh as he sets the

laundry basket on the floor and rubs Ziggy's head.

"This is Mae," I say. "She lives right next door. And that's Ziggy."

"Good to meet you. I'm Evan Taylor," Dad says.

"She brought cookies!" Malia says, still holding half of hers. "Snickerdoodles. Why are they called that, anyway? There aren't any Snickers in them."

"Just eat it," I tell her.

"Wow, thanks," Dad says to Mae. "My wife, Naomi, isn't home right now, but I'm sure she'll want to meet you, too."

Dad and Mae continue to make small talk while Malia and I sit on the floor next to Ziggy. He nuzzles his head under my hand, like he's asking me to pet him some more. When I do, he lets out a sound that's a mix between a sigh and a grunt. Malia strokes the smooth fur on his back.

"Look at that," Mae says. "Ziggy likes you."

"He's so sweet." Every time I stroke his fur, a little more of my stress melts away.

"We're only right next door, so anytime you want to come see Ziggy, just knock."

"Really?" I ask.

"Can I come, too?" Malia asks.

Mae smiles. "Of course. The little boy who lived here before you came by all the time. Ziggy loves children, but my grandkids live over an hour away, so he doesn't get as much time with them as he'd like. You'd be doing me a favor."

"Awesome," I say.

"Well, I don't want to impose for too long," Mae says.

"It's no problem," Dad says. "Everyone in this building has been really welcoming."

"There's a good community here," Mae says. "I used to live in a different building, where the people weren't nearly as friendly. They were more standoffish, always sticking to themselves. Never smiling back at me in the elevator. But here, people care about each other."

"Daddy, can I have another cookie?" Malia interrupts.

"One more and that's it," Dad tells her, and then says, "Yeah?" to Mae.

"Absolutely," Mae says. "When Sheila in 5F broke her leg, everybody pitched in to make her some frozen meals so she wouldn't have to be on her feet so much. And one of my good friends in the building, Monica, hosted a retirement party for me a few years back. Lots of people in the building came. It was very nice."

"That's great," Dad says.

Malia sits next to me again and hands me a second cookie, too. Ziggy immediately tries to sniff it, but I raise my arm so he can't reach. "Not for you, buddy," I tell him. He licks his lips and stares at the cookie as I take a bite.

"There are other dogs here, too," Mae says. "Not all buildings in the area allow dogs, because of the noise, but I couldn't live anywhere without Ziggy."

"He's pretty quiet," I say, thinking of all the sounds I've been hearing at night. "I wouldn't have guessed there was a dog next door. I haven't heard any barking."

"No, he's a good boy," Mae says. "And I always know exactly what he wants and needs, so he doesn't need to bark to get my attention.

"What do you do for work, Evan?" Mae asks Dad.

"Oh, well. I'm actually between jobs. I was laid off in January."

"That's terrible." Mae shakes her head and pauses to think. "What kind of work did you do? Maybe I know someone who can help. There might even be someone here in the building with a connection somewhere."

"I worked in telecommunications," Dad says. "They laid off thousands of employees. It was bad. I've been applying to other companies, even a few lower-level positions than what I had, but then I get rejected because they think I have too much experience."

"Ah," Mae says. "Well, I'll put out some feelers for you."

"Thank you," Dad says. "I appreciate that." He sounds more hopeful than I've heard him in a while. If he gets a new job, maybe we won't have to stay here for that long. We probably can't get our house back, but we can get another house like it. At the very least, maybe I'll be able to start my piano lessons again.

"Of course," Mae says.

"In the meantime, my brother is starting his own construction business," Dad says. "I'm thinking of partnering with him. Seems like working for yourself might be the way to go these days."

I don't think Mom would like hearing Dad say that, but I keep my mouth shut and go back to petting Ziggy. He licks my hand and then rests his head on my lap so I can keep scratching behind his ears.

"Anyway, if there's anything we can do for you, let us know," Dad says. "I'm around during most of the day, for now."

"Thank you." Mae stands up, says goodbye to us, and calls for Ziggy.

Once they've left, Dad says, "She was nice."

"Yeah," I say. Mae was really nice, but I keep thinking about how cute and lovable that dog was. "And Ziggy was so sweet."

"I think he's the cutest dog ever," Malia says.

I've heard of therapy dogs before, and now I understand. Ziggy was only here for a few minutes, but it was enough to get rid of all of the bad feelings inside me and replace them with warm and fuzzy ones.

Already, my lap is colder with him gone.

Chapter Six

On Friday night, Mom gets home early enough for all of us to eat dinner together. In our house, we used to always order takeout on Friday nights. Usually pizza, Thai food, or Chinese food. But since my parents are trying to save money, Dad cooks instead. We're having salmon that he baked in the oven, with a side of potatoes and broccoli. Everything tastes good, but it feels too healthy for a Friday night. I could go for an egg roll. Plus, I know I'm going to be able to smell fish for hours. So far, every time Mom or Dad have cooked something, even if they open the small window in the kitchen, the food smell is all over the apartment for hours later.

"How's it been taking the bus, Joy?" Dad asks.

"Fine. I've been sitting next to my new friend Nora. She's really nice. She's into movies, too, you know."

"That's great," Dad says.

Mom's cell phone rings. She grabs it and looks at the screen. "Be right back. I need to take this."

"You can't wait until we're done eating?" Dad asks.

"It'll only take a minute." Mom answers the call as she gets out of her seat. "Hi, Rachel? Uh-huh, hold on one second." She goes into my parents' bedroom and closes the door.

Dad's jaw hardens as he stands and goes into the kitchen. A second later, he's back with a bottle of hot sauce. He pours it aggressively over his food.

It's obvious Dad's mad, but I don't know what to say, so I take another bite of salmon.

Two minutes later, Mom comes back into the room. "See? I told you it wouldn't take long. It was my coworker. We have to give a presentation on Monday, so we need to finish working on it this weekend."

"When's work going to calm down again?" Dad asks as Mom sits back down and picks up her fork.

"What do you mean?" Mom asks.

"You never had to take so much work home before," Dad says.

"I wasn't trying to get a promotion before. And now I am. Which would mean a big pay increase that will help all of us."

"I get that," Dad begins. "It's just—"

"Do you get it?" Mom asks, cutting him off.

"Of course I do."

"I wouldn't be so stressed about getting this promotion if you took the hardware store job," Mom says under her breath.

"You know how I feel about that," Dad says. "I'm going to work with Spencer on getting his business up and running while I apply for other jobs."

"Well, you know how I feel about that," Mom says.

For what seems like the longest moment ever, the two of them glare at each other.

Then Dad glances over at me and Malia, who frowns as she picks at her potatoes. "Let's talk about this later," he says to Mom in a quieter voice.

"Fine," Mom says, not looking at him.

They go back to eating, and the next ten minutes are filled with awkward silence.

"May I be excused?" I finally ask when I can't take it anymore.

"Me too?" Malia asks.

"Sure," Mom says.

Malia and I pick up our plates and put them into the sink. We go into our room, and I close the door, but I can still hear them arguing.

"Why are they fighting so much?" Malia asks as she crawls onto her bed and hugs her stuffed narwhal.

"I don't know," I tell her. "But I'm sure it'll be fine."

"You promise?" Malia asks.

I go over to her bed and put my pinkie out. "Pinkie promise."

We link pinkies, and Malia smiles.

I'm only saying this so she won't worry, but I don't know if I believe it.

The dinner churns in my stomach. I don't know how to make my parents get along, and there's nothing I can do about living in this apartment. But I can't stand for things to stay like this—for all of us to be so unhappy.

I'm about to crawl up to my top bunk and turn on the *Black Panther* soundtrack when our doorbell rings. I immediately think of Ziggy. Maybe Mae is back with some more cookies. Malia and I peek into the hallway as Mom is opening the door.

It's not Ziggy. It's Nora.

"Hi, I'm Nora from upstairs, 5B. Is Joy here?"

"Oh hi. I'm Joy's mom."

I walk toward the front door. "Hey."

Mom steps out of the way, and Nora comes inside. She sniffs at the air. "Did you have salmon for dinner? It smells yummy."

I groan because *how embarrassing*, but Mom says, "Actually, we did."

Nora smiles.

"What's up?" I ask, hoping Mom will get the hint and leave us alone.

"If you're not busy, want to come over and watch a movie?" Nora asks. "We can pick something on demand."

"That sounds fun," I say. "Mom, can I go?"

"You're only going upstairs?" Mom asks.

"Yup," Nora says. "If you want, you can follow us to my place and meet my dad."

"Okay," Mom says. "I'll let Joy's dad know what's going on." She turns and walks back toward her bedroom.

"You have the best timing. I could use a break from"—I gesture—"all of this."

"All of what?" Nora frowns a little. "Is everything okay?"

"Yeah, I just . . ." I don't get to finish my sentence because Mom comes back in. "I'll tell you later," I whisper to Nora.

"Ready to go?" Mom asks.

"Yup," Nora says.

"Wait one second." I go into the kitchen and grab two of Mae's cookies from the Tupperware. "Here." I hand Nora one. "Mae from next door made them."

"Yesss," Nora says, and takes a bite.

"I got to meet her dog, Ziggy," I add. "He's so cute."

"I know, right? He has the cutest, squishiest face."

Mom and I follow her two floors up to her apartment.

Nora lets us inside, and I'm hit with the scent of buttered popcorn. It smells delicious and makes me a little less insecure about our apartment smelling like food. It's not only us. The popcorn smells much better than the fish, though, and my mouth immediately waters.

Nora's dad is sitting on the couch next to her little sister, who's reading a copy of One Crazy Summer.

He stands up when he sees us. "Hi, Joy," he says to me. To Mom, he says, "You must be her mom. Great to meet you. I'm Felix." He points to Nora's sister. "That's my little bookworm, Izzy, over there."

"I'm Naomi," Mom says. "Nice to meet you, too. Nora says it's okay if Joy watches a movie?"

"Absolutely," Felix says.

They exchange phone numbers and then Mom leaves.

"Popcorn's in the kitchen," Felix says. "Shout if you need anything. Izzy, why don't you finish reading in your room."

Izzy reluctantly gets up from her cozy spot on the couch and follows her dad down the hallway.

When they're gone, Nora goes into the kitchen. I stand in the doorway and watch as she pours the popcorn from the microwave bag into a large bowl. "What do you want to drink? We have regular water and flavored seltzer. Dad won't let us drink real soda."

"I'll take a flavored seltzer," I say.

She peers into the fridge. "Grapefruit or lemon-lime?"

"Grapefruit."

Nora grabs the drinks, and I take the bowl back into the living room. I kick my shoes off, and we get comfy on the couch.

"Should we pick a movie?" Nora asks. "Or . . . do you want to talk about what you said downstairs?"

"Um. Well, I guess things have been stressful lately," I say. "With the move. And my parents have been fighting more and more—arguments about money and stuff."

"Oh," Nora says. "That stinks."

"Yeah. It's hard to escape it when we're right on top of each other in the apartment. Malia and I can hear practically everything." I pause. "That reminds me. What were you talking about the other day? About a place to escape?"

Nora scoots closer to me on the couch and lowers her voice. "Can you keep a secret?"

"Of course," I tell her.

"You have to promise not to tell any grown-ups. Not your parents. Not my dad. Not Carlos the super. *Nobody.*"

I mime zipping my lips shut. "I promise I won't tell anyone."

Nora smiles. "Put your shoes back on."

"Wait, we're going there now?" I ask.

"You want to see it, don't you?"

"Yeah," I say, even though I'm a little nervous. She hasn't even told me what this place is, and she wants me to follow her there? But I'm too curious not to, so I slip my sneakers back on.

"Dad!" Nora yells toward the small hallway leading to the bedrooms. "Joy has laundry downstairs, so I'm going to go with her to put it in the dryer. Be back in a few!" To me, she whispers, "So he won't go looking for us."

"Okay!" Felix yells back.

Nora opens her front door and glances back at me. "Let's go."

Chapter Seven

My mind races as I follow Nora downstairs. Where is she taking me? Is it in the building or outside somewhere?

The lobby is empty and eerily quiet. This is my first time coming down here at night, and it's giving me goose bumps.

Then Nora stops at a door in the hallway that leads to the laundry room. She opens it and clicks on the light. Peering inside, I realize it's a storage closet. It's a decent-sized room, with a row of shelves along one wall holding different cleaning supplies. On the floor right next to the door is a bucket and mop. In one corner, I see what looks like a bag holding an artificial Christmas tree.

Is this it? This can't be the super-secret room Nora's been hinting at. I know I said I wanted a place to escape, but I don't want to hang out in a closet full of cleaning stuff.

"Come in, quick. And close the door behind you," Nora says.

I do as she says. With the door closed, I notice the faint scent of bleach and artificial lemon in the air.

"Um . . . this isn't . . . ," I start to say.

"No, silly," Nora says. "Come back here."

She leads me to the back of the closet and around a corner. That's when I realize this closet is shaped like an L. Back here, there are a bunch of boxes.

Nora points to the floor. "There."

I look down, not sure what she's pointing at. But then I see it. In the wood floor is the outline of a square. And on one side of the square is . . . *is that a handle?*

Before I can ask, Nora lifts it and pulls. It's a door! Nora opens it all the way until the door is standing up, leaning against the wall next to it. I peer inside and see a set of old brick stairs leading down.

I have to admit, it's a little spooky. It seems like this could be the beginning of a horror movie. Girl walks down creepy stairs in the back of a smelly storage closet, and she is never seen again.

I gulp. "You're, um, sure it's safe?"

"Of course!" Nora says. "Follow me." She turns on her phone's flashlight, and I do the same. She carefully walks down the stairs, which wind around a corner. I let her go a few steps before following her.

"Close the door behind you," Nora says.

"You sure?" I ask. "We won't be locked in?"

"Stop worrying!" Nora says from the bottom of the stairs.

I close the door and go down the stairs to meet her.

"Here we are," Nora says, turning around to face me. "Welcome to the Hideout."

My mouth drops as I stare past her. It's a room, sort of like the unfinished basement in my old house. Except this is much nicer. The floor has a colorful rug on it, and there are Christmas lights strung around the space. There's a single light bulb in the middle of the ceiling, with a paper lantern around it, giving the room a warm glow. And the walls are all decorated. On one wall, someone hung a fabric mural. It looks like it was hand-made from a white sheet. It has all sorts of colorful paint designs on it: paint splatters, handprints, circles, hearts, rainbows. It's beautiful.

There's a small window on the top of the wall on

one side. Right underneath it is a bookshelf with some books and old-school board games, like Twister, Connect Four, and Operation. I also spot Taboo, Scattergories, and Monopoly.

On the other walls, there are doodles and handwritten messages in different-colored markers. I go up close and read some of them.

JACKSON WAS HERE.
WHAT HAPPENS IN THE HIDEOUT STAYS IN THE HIDEOUT.
MOLLY + ESME = BFFAE

I recognize some song lyrics from the *Hamilton* musical. There's also a ton of drawings and illustrations.

"Wow" is all I can say.

"I knew you'd like it," Nora says. When I turn to face her, she's grinning.

"What *is* this place?" I ask.

"It's a secret Hideout, just for the kids in the building."

"Wait, so no adults know about it?"

Nora shakes her head. "That's the number one rule for this place. We can't let adults find out about it."

"How did *you* find out about it?"

Nora sits down on one of the two beanbag chairs next to the bookshelf. I sit on the other one.

"Another kid who used to live here, Will, showed it to me," Nora explains. "And someone else showed it to him. Ten years ago, this kid, Peter, discovered it. He was the son of the super back then. One day, he was hiding in the storage closet upstairs during a game of hide-and-seek, and he found the door. He opened it and saw the stairs leading down. At first, he was freaked out, so he got two of his friends, and they decided to check it out together. Anyway, when they realized there was a room down here that nobody else seemed to know about, they decided to make it their own. They started bringing their own stuff down and inviting other kids to hang out."

"Wow," I say again. "That is so cool." This Hideout really is the perfect escape. I can come down here when I need a break from my parents fighting, or when I miss having my own room.

"I know, right?" Nora says. "I knew you'd love it. I come down here when I want space from my sister or dad. Sometimes I'll read or draw, or sometimes Oliver, Elena, and Miles are down here, too. We'll play games or talk about stuff."

"That sounds so fun. I have a million questions!"

Nora laughs. "You look like me when I first came down here. I'll give you every answer I know. But we should probably head back upstairs so my dad doesn't wonder where we are."

I don't want to leave yet, but I know Nora is right.

Nora turns off all the lights, and we head back up the stairs. Before we go back into the hallway, Nora checks to make sure the coast is clear.

Back in Nora's apartment, we turn on a movie, but it plays in the background as Nora and I whisper to each other, and she tells me more about the Hideout. Like how she hasn't told her little sister about it yet, but she plans to tell her when she gets to middle school. I decide not to tell Malia about it either. It'll be nice to have a place to escape without her, and she can't keep a secret anyway.

Nora also says that the only other rule is we all have to keep it clean. We can't leave food down there, or let it get too dusty or gross. Everyone pitches in, and it helps to have a cleaning supply closet right upstairs.

It's so easy to talk to Nora, but eventually we start watching the movie for real. When it's over, I say goodbye and head back to 3C. Malia, who has an earlier bedtime, is already asleep. When I say good night to my parents, only Mom is in their room.

"Where's Dad?" I ask.

"He's staying at your uncle Spencer's place tonight."

"Why?"

"He just needs some space," Mom says. "It's nothing to worry about."

Some space. He wouldn't need space if we hadn't moved here.

With that, the good mood I've had, from hanging out with Nora and seeing the Hideout, vanishes into thin air.

Chapter Eight

Dad's not home from Uncle Spencer's when I wake up the next morning. Or when Malia and I eat bowls of cereal on the couch while watching cartoons. On Saturday mornings Dad usually makes the best breakfasts: fluffy buttermilk pancakes, cheesy eggs, and crispy bacon. While he and Mom drink coffee, Malia and I have hot chocolate with mini marshmallows. After we eat, Dad always watches cartoons with us.

But not today. It's not the same with only Malia and me—and cold cereal.

"Where'd Daddy go?" Malia asks. "He's missing the cartoons." She already has her ballet outfit on—a pink leotard, pink tights, and a pink tutu. Her hair is in two poufs. She looks adorable.

I don't want to tell her that he didn't sleep at home, and make her worry. "He went over to help Uncle Spencer with something." It's not entirely wrong, since that's probably where he still is.

"Oh," Malia says, sounding disappointed. But then she goes back to watching her favorite cartoon.

I look down at my cereal bowl, no longer hungry. Is this how it's going to be from now on? Will Dad always leave whenever he wants? It's like everything normal is crumbling around me, one by one.

When I bring my cereal bowl back to the kitchen, Mom's in there pouring milk into a steaming mug of coffee. "When's Dad coming back home?" I ask her.

"He should be back this afternoon." She glances at the clock on the microwave and then goes into the living room. "Malia, finish your cereal. It's almost time for ballet."

Usually I have a piano lesson at the same time as Malia's ballet class. The music school is right next to the ballet school. Now what will I do? I don't want to hang out at the ballet studio with Mom. I don't want to see the other kids walking into the music school with their instruments. Maybe Mom will let me stay home, and I can go back down to the Hideout. I was hoping to hang out with Nora again. I found a new song from a movie that I think she'll like.

But then Mom comes back and says, "Malia has a play-date after ballet. Want to go to the Crêperie while she's gone? We can share your favorite crêpe."

"Really?" The Crêperie is one of my favorite restaurants, but we haven't been there in a while—not since before my parents had to put our house up for sale. Just the thought of my favorite crêpe—strawberry and banana with Nutella, powdered sugar, and whipped cream—makes my mouth water.

"Really," Mom says. "We haven't had a lot of time lately to hang out, just the two of us."

"You've been busy," I say.

Mom gives a sad sigh. "I know. Trust me, I wish I weren't so busy, especially with work. But it's the way things need to be right now." She smiles. "So, crêpe?"

I bet Mom is only offering to take me there because she feels bad that I can't take my piano lesson. But a consolation crêpe will still be yummy. I smile back. "Okay."

"Great."

A half hour later, we drop Malia off at the ballet studio to meet her friend and her mom. Then Mom drives us to the restaurant.

On the way, I keep thinking that I need to do something. Money seems to be the root of all of our problems. It's why we had to move in the first place, and why my parents keep fighting now. Maybe there's something I can do to make some money, to help out until Dad can find a new job. He doesn't want to only make seven bucks an hour, but I'm more than okay with making that much. That way I could help pay for groceries or Malia's and my school supplies.

Maybe I could even make enough to pay for piano lessons. If I can save up enough for a semester of lessons at the music school, then Mom and Dad would have to agree to let me take them.

Maybe I could take the job at the hardware store, since Dad doesn't want it. I know I'm only a kid, but I'm sure I could handle it. I'm a hard worker when I want to be.

When we get to the Crêperie, I don't need to look at the menu since I know exactly what I want to order. Mom does, too. She orders my favorite crêpe and an iced latte for herself.

"Do you think Dad will get a new job?" I ask after the waitress takes our orders.

"I'm sure he will," Mom says. "The real question is when. Hopefully sooner rather than later."

"When am I allowed to get a job?" I ask. "Like work in a store, for instance?"

"I think you have to be fourteen. Maybe older."

I won't be fourteen for another year and a half. I frown. There goes my plan.

"Why do you want to know?" Mom asks.

I shrug. "I was thinking I could get a job. Maybe work at the hardware store, since Dad doesn't want to."

Mom reaches over and squeezes my hand. "Oh, honey. Don't worry about that. We're going to be fine. Focus on being a kid and having fun. And eating this crêpe."

She says that as the waitress returns with a big round plate that has a delicately folded crêpe on top. I breathe in the smell of warm Nutella, fruit, and sugar.

"Why don't we check out the thrift store after this?" Mom says, once I start eating. "I want to spruce up our apartment, make it feel more like home. But on a tiny budget. I have a list of ideas."

"Can I help?" I ask. At our old house, Mom used to love watching HGTV, the channel with all the home improvement shows. Sometimes I'd sit and watch with her. My favorite shows were the makeover ones, where the designer would fix up a room and do a big reveal at the end.

"Of course." Mom smiles. "That would be fun."

I take my time finishing the crêpe, savoring every last bite. Who knows when I'll get to come back here with Mom?

Then she drives us to the thrift store. As soon as we get inside, I see it—a beautiful, shiny, wooden upright piano. I can't believe it. It's standing right there in the middle of the store, with a bench underneath it. I walk right up to it and run my fingers across some of the keys. It needs to be tuned, but it sounds good.

How perfect is this! My parents said they couldn't afford a piano, but this is a thrift store, so it can't be that expensive.

Mom stands next to me. "Wow. I didn't think they'd have a piano here. It looks like it's in decent shape, too. I love the details."

She's talking about the carved wood details on the legs and on the ledge where the sheet music goes. It's a gorgeous piano. I could totally imagine it against the wall in my bedroom.

"Can we get it?" I ask Mom. "Please? A used piano is definitely cheaper than a brand-new one."

She looks at the price sticker and frowns. "It's nice, and six hundred dollars seems like a good deal. But we can't spend this much right now, sweetie."

Even though I shouldn't be surprised she said no, I'm

just as crushed as the first time.

"This stinks," I mumble.

"I know," Mom says. "I'm sorry."

If I were allowed to get a job, I could save up to buy this piano myself. But six hundred dollars is a lot of money. Even if I were able to make seven dollars an hour, it'd take me forever to save up, and by then, this piano would probably be gone. I should think smaller. Like a keyboard. Those are much cheaper, and it could work in the short term if I can save up enough for lessons. And they're always available online. I could even wait for a sale. Then, when Dad gets a new job and my parents aren't stressing about money so much, I can get a real piano like this one.

There's got to be a job that I can do as a twelve-year-old. There's babysitting, though I don't think I'd enjoy that much. Maybe I can tutor? I'm pretty good at math.

I decide to do some online research when I get home. No matter what Mom said, I'm determined to figure out something that I can do to make money.

For the first time in a while, I'm optimistic. Like I'm taking control of something, even if I don't have it all figured out yet.

Chapter Nine

The day has come. I reach for Mae's Tupperware container, which we've kept at the top of the fridge ever since the night she brought over the cookies. I've finally reached the last snickerdoodle. I savor every last cinnamon-sugary bite.

I wash and dry the container and then go out into the hallway. I bet she needs it back, and it's also a good excuse to see Ziggy again. I press on Mae's doorbell, and a minute later, she opens the door. Ziggy is at her heels, and when he sees me, he wags his tail.

"Hi, Joy," Mae says.

"Hi!" I lean over to pet Ziggy and let him lick my

hand. I rub his head and behind his soft ears.

When I stand up again, I notice Mae is holding a cane. "Did you hurt your leg or something?" I frown.

"My knee," she explains. "It's been bothering me more and more lately. I have to start physical therapy."

"Oh no, I'm sorry," I say.

"Just a sign of getting older." She shrugs. "I feel bad for Ziggy, though. I haven't been able to take him on many walks lately. I can bring him downstairs to do his business on the grass in front of the building, but that's about it for now."

I look down at Ziggy, who stares up at me like he's excited to have someone new around. I bet he's been stuck in the apartment a lot.

"Do you want me to walk him for you?" I ask.

"Oh. No, I couldn't make you do that."

"It'd be fun. I'm pretty sure my parents won't let me get a dog of my own. And I really like Ziggy." I give him another scratch behind his ears.

"Well, if you're interested, I'd pay you of course," Mae says. "I was actually thinking that I should go ahead and hire a dog walker to come by."

"No way, you don't have to pay me." The words automatically spill out.

Wait a minute. What am I saying? I think about my piano

lessons, and the keyboard I'm dying to save up for. If Mae pays me, then this will be a real job. A real job I can have now, instead of waiting until I'm fourteen. "I mean," I say. "Well, actually, if you were going to pay someone else anyway . . . I could use the money."

Mae laughs. "Of course. I would never expect you to do something like this for free. Keep that in mind for the future, Joy. Don't ever let anyone take advantage of you."

I nod. "I have to ask my parents if it's okay with them."

"Of course. Let me know what they say. I'm here if they want to talk to me about it."

I smile, not able to believe my luck. "Bye for now," I tell Mae.

I head back to my apartment. Dad is in the kitchen, washing dishes, and Mom is in our room, helping Malia with homework. By the time Mom and I got home from the thrift store yesterday, Dad was back from Uncle Spencer's house. We all ate dinner together last night, and Dad didn't leave again, but I've noticed Mom and Dad haven't been talking to each other much. At least not in front of me and Malia. Anything is better than them fighting. Maybe one night away was all Dad needed. Maybe Uncle Spencer's house will be like the Hideout—a temporary place to go when he needs some space.

I decide to ask Dad about the dog walking first. He

loves dogs, so I have a feeling he'll be on board.

"Ziggy seems like a great dog," he says, once I've recapped my conversation with Mae. "But I don't know. I'm sorry about Mae's knee, but walking someone else's dog is a pretty big responsibility."

"It's a responsibility, yeah," I say. "But not too big for me. I know I can handle it."

"Does your mom know about this yet?"

I shake my head. "Not yet."

Dad wipes his wet hands off on a dish towel. "Let's see what she thinks." He leaves the kitchen and returns with Mom.

"What's up?" she asks.

"I was talking to Mae next door," I say. "She needs help walking her dog, Ziggy, until her knee gets better. Can I do it? She says she'll pay me to walk him."

Please say yes, I think as I watch Mom take in what I've said.

"I don't know," Mom says. "You've never done anything like this before."

"I take walks all the time. It's basically the same thing, except I'll be holding a dog's leash."

"Right, I know," Mom says. "But you've never been responsible for another person's pet before. It's going to involve more than walking, and you aren't usually around dogs." She pauses. "We'll think about it."

"But Mae needs someone to walk Ziggy *now*." Now that Mae has it in her head that she wants to hire a dog walker, I need to make sure she hires *me* and not somebody else.

"Your mom and I will talk about it some more later, okay?" Dad says. "We'll get an answer to you soon."

"Fine," I mumble.

Why is it that the only times Mom and Dad agree lately, it's about something that I want? I need to find a way to convince them both that I can do this, that I'm the best person for this job.

I need to come up with a plan.

Chapter Ten

To come up with a good plan, I need a place to think. The Hideout pops into my head, but my parents won't let me leave our apartment without telling them where I'm going. What reason can I give them? It's raining, so I can't tell them that I want to go for a walk.

I grab my phone and text Nora.

JOY: Hi!

JOY: What do you usually tell your parents when you want to go to the Hideout?

Three dots appear on the screen as Nora starts typing on her end.

NORA: Depends
NORA: But I'm not doing anything right now
NORA: I can meet you and then we can tell our parents we are at each other's apts!
JOY: Ok! See you down there

I'm excited to hang out with Nora again, and in the Hideout. Maybe she can help me with my dog-walking dilemma.

And then it hits me. *Nora!* Maybe she can walk Ziggy with me. Mom and Dad think it's too big of a responsibility for just me, but with two of us, they'd have to let us do it.

My parents don't blink an eye when I ask to hang out at Nora's apartment. I feel bad about lying, but they aren't supposed to know the Hideout exists. How else can I spend time down there? At least I'm still inside the building. I take the stairs to the first floor and find Nora in the hallway next to the storage closet.

But she isn't alone. She's talking to a woman who has a tall, black rolling cart next to her that overflows with bags of laundry.

Nora waves when she sees me. To the woman, she says, "Mrs. Martinez, have you met Joy yet?"

"I don't think so." Mrs. Martinez turns to me. "Nice to meet you, Joy. You can call me Daniela. Though Nora always insists on calling me Mrs. Martinez." She laughs.

"Joy just moved into 3C," Nora says, confirming that people here really do want to know each other's apartment numbers. Or maybe it's a Nora thing.

Daniela's face flashes with recognition. "I met your parents when you all moved in last week. My husband, Carlos, is the building's super. If you need anything at all, you can go to him. We're in 1A."

"Thanks," I say.

"You might also see my little ones running around," Daniela says. "There's Sofia, Mateo, and Victoria." She points to her cart and laughs. "That's why I have so much laundry."

"Her kids are super cute," Nora says.

I smile. Nora and Mae were right—everyone in this building is super friendly.

"I better get started," Daniela says. "Have a good afternoon, girls."

"See ya," Nora says.

Nora and I watch as Daniela rolls her cart down the hallway to the laundry room. As soon as she's out of sight,

Nora opens the storage closet and pulls me inside, closing the door behind her.

"That was close," Nora says. "I was about to go into the closet when Mrs. Mart—I mean, Daniela—came around the corner. But then before I could come up with an excuse, she started talking to me about something else."

"Wow," I say. "Does this happen a lot—you almost getting caught?"

"Sometimes. But sneaking around is part of the fun." She smiles. "Let's get down to the Hideout before Carlos or someone else comes in here looking for cleaning supplies."

I follow Nora to the Hideout door, and we slip inside. When we get downstairs, Nora turns on all of the lights—since with the rain, no sunshine is coming through the one small window in the room.

"I can't get over how cool it looks in here, especially with the Christmas lights," I say.

"Christmas lights make every room look better," Nora says.

"Maybe I should put some around my room upstairs." As soon as I say it, I decide to make it happen. It'll make our room so much cozier.

Nora plops down on a blue beanbag chair. I sit down

on the other one and get comfortable.

"Anyway, how are things?" Nora asks.

"They're okay." I think about telling Nora about my dad not sleeping at home on Friday night, but I don't want to talk about that right now. There are more important things on my mind. "Actually, I have a proposition for you."

Nora leans in closer to me and says, "Go on . . ."

I explain that Mae is willing to pay me to walk Ziggy, but my parents don't want me to walk a dog by myself.

"Do you want to walk him with me?" I ask. "I'll give you half of the money. You could put it toward the new camera you want."

"Are you serious?" Nora asks.

"Yeah!" It would be nice to have all the money to myself, but this way I might actually get the job. I'll still get to save up for piano lessons and a keyboard. It'll just take me a little longer.

Plus, it'll be fun to spend some more one-on-one time with Nora. We have our bus rides, and I started eating lunch with her and her friends. All of the broadcasting club kids are nice, but they're also really talkative, so mostly I eat and listen.

"That sounds fun!" Nora says. "Ziggy is so stinking cute. I see Mae taking him outside sometimes."

"I'm so excited," I say. "Now we have to tell our parents we want to do it together. Do you think your dad will let you?"

"I'm pretty sure I can convince him. Usually, when I really want something, I go to him with a list of arguments. So he can't refuse."

As soon as she says the word "list," I know I made the right choice in asking Nora. "I love lists."

"Me too! One sec." Nora gets up.

While she rummages through a small bin on the bookshelf, I stare at the doodles on the wall next to me. Someone drew a picture of the apartment building with the Hideout underneath it, looking like the tunnels prairie dogs burrow in. In red marker, they put a heart in the middle of the Hideout.

Nora plops back down on her beanbag chair, holding a piece of paper and markers. She uses the Monopoly box as a table. "We can use this to write down our argument, and then present it to both of our parents. Make it so they can't say no."

I smile. "I like how you think."

Nora uncaps the red marker and, in bold letters at the top of the page, writes: "Reasons Joy and Nora Should Be Allowed to Walk Ziggy."

I get an idea and grab the black marker from her. Under

the header, I write: "We'll spend less time watching TV."

"Good one." Next, she writes, "It'll increase our happiness."

We spend the next half hour writing down more reasons, like "We'll learn to become more responsible," "We'll get more exercise," "We'll be helping out a neighbor," and "We'll learn how to earn and save our own money."

Once the list is complete, we decide to draw a picture on the bottom of the two of us with Ziggy in between. Nora draws us with big smiles. I draw Ziggy, and also some scenery, like grass, a sidewalk, and a tree. And then Nora draws a piggy bank with dollar signs around it.

"We should've gotten Oliver to come down here and help us with this part," Nora says, staring at our illustration.

I think of Oliver drawing in his sketchbook every day on the bus to school.

"It's not that bad." I laugh. It's not that great, either, but it'll have to do.

"Can you think of anything else we should add?" I ask.

Nora skims our list again. "Nope. Wanna show it to our parents? I'll go see if my dad can come over to your place, so we can talk to them all together."

"Okay."

We turn off the lights and sneak back out of the Hideout, checking the hallway outside the storage closet first to make sure nobody is around.

As we're walking to the elevator, we run into Elena.

"Hey! I'm going to the Hideout." She lowers her voice when she says the word "Hideout." "Want to come and play a board game?"

"We'd love to, but there's something we have to do," Nora says. "Another time? We should plan another game night."

"Definitely!" Elena says.

We say goodbye to Elena and head to the elevator.

"Game night?" I ask Nora.

"Oh yeah. Sometimes we all get together in the Hideout to play games and eat snacks. It's super fun."

"Sounds fun. By the way, thanks for showing me the Hideout. And, um, for letting me into your friend group. I was really nervous my first day at the bus stop."

Nora smiles at me. "You're one of us now."

I smile back, but as soon as we get upstairs, my palms get sweaty. I hope our dog-walking plan works. The last thing I need is more disappointment.

Chapter Eleven

Sharing our list with our parents sounded like a much better idea before we were actually standing in front of the three of them in my living room. They're staring at us with curious expressions. Meanwhile, I might throw up.

I look over at Nora, who doesn't seem nervous at all. She smiles and says, "Thank you all for being here." Then she looks at me.

Right. This is my part.

"Um, we brought you here so we can talk about the dog-walking job that Mae offered me."

Why didn't I get water first? My throat is so dry. I clear it and continue.

"I talked to Nora, and she said she'll walk Ziggy with me, if it's . . . if her dad says it's okay."

My mom starts to talk, but Nora puts her hand up. "Please. Before you say anything, we want to show you this."

She nods at me, and I hold up our list so our parents can see it. "These are the reasons why we should be allowed to walk Ziggy."

Nora and I go back and forth, each reading a different argument from the list. I watch our parents' faces as we present each argument, but I can't tell what they're thinking.

Finally, we get to the end. "So . . . what do you think?" I ask, bracing myself for the worst.

Mom, Dad, and Felix look at each other, but don't say anything. Then Mom says, "Why don't you girls go check on Malia and Izzy, and let us talk for a minute?"

"Okay." I lead Nora back to my room, where our sisters are splayed out on the floor, surrounded by markers, stickers, and paper. They're hard at work making drawings and barely seem to notice that we've come in.

"How do you think it went?" I ask.

Nora shrugs. "I have no idea."

I stand near my bedroom door to see if I can hear what our parents are saying, but they're talking too low.

Ten minutes later, Dad comes back and tells us they're ready to share their decision.

My heart pounds so loud, it's like the beating drums from *Jumanji*.

"We thought about everything you said," Felix says. "First of all, we appreciate the time you took to write down all of the reasons why you want to do this. It tells us how important this is to you."

Oh my gosh, get to it! I want to scream.

Mom must see the desperation in my face, because she says, "We're going to let you walk Ziggy."

"Really?" I ask.

"They said yes!" Nora hugs me.

"Thank you so much," I say, laughing.

"We already talked to Mae, and worked it out with her," Mom says. "You two can walk Ziggy once a day, Monday through Friday, and then twice a day on the weekends. She'll pay forty dollars, so each of you will get twenty dollars a week. But you have to stay on our street or within the park behind the building when you walk him. And you must keep your phones with you at all times."

"We promise!" I say.

"You can start tomorrow," Mom says.

This is the best news ever!

Felix gets up from the couch. "We should probably get going so I can make dinner. Nora, tell Izzy it's time to go."

When they're gone, I thank Mom and Dad again. "You won't regret this. I can even give you some of the money for stuff around the house."

"Absolutely not," Mom says. "I know we don't have as much as we used to, but we're fine. Whatever money you make, you should use for yourself."

"Are you sure?" I ask.

"Yes," Mom says. "I insist."

I can't stop smiling. I officially have my first job!

After school the next day, Nora and I get off the bus, drop our backpacks off in our apartments, and then meet outside Mae's door.

"Hi, girls," Mae says as she answers it. Ziggy is at her feet, wagging his tail, like he already knows he's getting a walk. It's probably because he's got his harness and leash on.

Mae hands us the leash and a tote bag. "This has some plastic baggies to clean up after him. There're also some treats, and I threw in a couple of water bottles."

We thank Mae and tell her we'll be back soon.

While we wait for the elevator, I say, "You know, I

completely forgot about the picking-up-poop part." I laugh.

"I remembered," Nora says. "But don't worry. With the bags Mae gave us, we won't actually have to touch the poop. I brought hand sanitizer anyway, though, to be safe."

I hold Ziggy's leash as we head outside. I can tell he's happy to be able to actually walk down the street, instead of just peeing on the patch of grass in front of the building. He wags his tail happily as we walk, and he starts leading the way, pulling on the leash in my hand.

"Whoa, Ziggy." I tighten my grip. "Guess you know exactly where you want to go, bud."

Thankfully Ziggy seems to be leading us straight to the park. A few times along the way, he stops to lift his leg and pee on bushes.

"How's your screenplay going?" I ask Nora.

"Good! I only have a few more scenes to write, but then I have to go back and fix a lot of stuff."

"It's so cool that you're writing your own movie."

"Thanks. I'm proud of it so far."

We arrive at the park, and Ziggy stops pulling his leash as much. That is, until he spots a squirrel, and then he starts jumping up and down and yelping, like he would love more than anything in the world to be free to chase it.

"No, Ziggy! Let's pull him this way," I suggest to Nora.

"Want me to hold the leash for a while?" she asks.

"Sure." I hand it to her.

We start walking around the main path in the park.

"I've always wanted a dog," Nora says. "My mom had one growing up. They're in a lot of her pictures. If she was still around, we'd probably have one by now."

"Would your dad get you one?"

"The last time I asked, he said he didn't want the extra responsibility. But maybe if I walk dogs for a while, I can convince him that I can handle it."

"What kind of dog would you want?"

"My mom had a corgi, so maybe one of those?"

"What do corgis look like?"

Nora stops walking and gets out her phone. Ziggy pulls on the leash, clearly not ready to stop. "One sec, Zig," Nora says as she types into her phone and then holds it out to me.

"Oh my gosh, so cute!" I say as I stare at a picture of a small dog with big ears and short legs.

"Right?"

Ziggy pulls at the leash again and whines.

"Okay, okay, we're going," Nora says, and we start walking again.

We only make it a little farther before Ziggy pauses by a bush.

"This is what you were whining for?" I ask him. "A bush?"

Ziggy sniffs it a whole lot, paws at the ground a bit, and turns around in a few circles.

Then he starts to poop.

Oh.

I don't want to stare at Ziggy while he's doing his thing, so I look at Nora. I guess Nora doesn't want to watch Ziggy either, because she looks at me. We stare at each other for a second, both looking uncertain. And then we burst out laughing. I start tearing up from laughing so hard, and Nora covers her mouth. Meanwhile, Ziggy finishes doing his business and looks up at us, like he's both proud of what he's done and confused by how we're behaving. This only makes us laugh even more.

"So, uh, who should pick up the first poop?" I ask, once we've calmed down. "You want to do the honors?"

"No, you should," Nora says. "Since, you know, we wouldn't have this dog-walking job if it wasn't for you."

"How about we Rock Paper Scissors to decide?" I suggest. "Best two out of three?"

"Okay."

"Rock. Paper. Scissors. Shoot," we say at the same time. I throw rock, and Nora throws paper.

"Rock. Paper. Scissors. Shoot," we say again. I throw scissors, and Nora throws paper again, so I win.

"All right, next loser gets the poop," Nora says.

"Rock. Paper. Scissors. Shoot," we say for the last time. I throw paper, and Nora throws scissors.

"Yes!" She does a happy dance.

"Fine, I'll get the first one." I grab the poop bags out of Mae's tote bag. "But we're switching off, so you get the next one."

"Fair."

I pick it up as quickly as I can, and we find a trash can so I can throw it away.

"Good job," Nora says.

She hands me her bottle of hand sanitizer, and I squirt the hugest blob into my palm.

I smile, glad that we're doing this together.

Chapter Twelve

Ziggy runs right inside as soon as Mae opens her door.

"Thank you again for doing this," she says as I hand back her tote bag.

Ziggy returns with water dripping off his chin. He's panting a little, and with his tongue sticking out, it's like he's one of those smiling emojis.

"I can tell Ziggy had a good time," Mae adds.

"It was a lot of fun!" I say.

I leave Mae's with the biggest smile on my face. Our parents had no reason to doubt us, and now I'm one step closer to taking piano lessons again.

That excitement disappears as soon as I open our apartment door. Nobody is in the living room, but from the entryway, I can hear Mom and Dad back in their room, arguing. Their voices are clear, even with their bedroom door closed. I kick off my shoes and head into my room to check on Malia. She's lying across the bottom bunk.

"Hey," I say.

Malia looks up from her tablet, which has a puzzle game open. "They're yelling again," she says, her voice small. "It's scaring me."

I sit next to her on the bed. "I can hear that. But don't worry," I say automatically. "It'll be okay." I put my pinkie out, and she links hers. I wiggle our hands, which makes her smile.

"Do you want a snack?" I ask. "I can make us something."

Malia sits up. "Are there any peanut butter crackers?"

"I'll check." I bring Malia into the living room and turn the TV on to drown out my parents. Back in our house, they never let Malia have this much screen time. But they also weren't too busy arguing to pay attention to her.

I find Malia's favorite peanut butter crackers in a

kitchen cabinet. I like them, too, but there's no way I can eat anything right now.

No matter what I say to Malia, I know we're far from okay.

I should still be thinking about how great the first walk with Ziggy went, but instead I keep thinking about how much my parents are fighting, and how different everything is now.

I wish we were back in our real home, where Mom and Dad got along.

I miss our house. The feel of the wooden steps under my bare feet when I'd walk downstairs in the mornings and the smooth railing under my fingertips.

Like on Christmas morning. Before Malia and I even got all the way down the stairs, we'd see our huge, beautiful tree that we'd decorated together. The presents were always nice, but being together—with the fireplace going, and Dad's favorite Motown Christmas album playing—was the best part. I wish I'd known that last Christmas would be our last in the house. But maybe it's better that I didn't know.

Will we even be able to fit a Christmas tree in this apartment? There's not a lot of space.

Will Mom and Dad be able to stop fighting long enough for us to enjoy Christmas, or any holiday, together?

I don't want to think about that, so I open the list on my phone of things I'll miss about my old house, and read through the memories I want to remember.

The beautiful light that streamed into our kitchen in the early evenings, which Mom called "magic hour."

The window over the sink overlooking the backyard. Mom used to put a glass jar on its ledge with clippings from the hydrangea bush next to the garage.

The quiet hum of the house.

The bird sounds from outside when we opened the windows.

The smell of fresh-cut grass when Dad mowed the lawn.

More than anything, I miss the feeling of being home. I belonged there. I'm not sure I'll ever belong here.

I feel heartbroken.

Will this heaviness in my chest ever go away?

After dinner, I use Nora as an excuse again so I can go down to the Hideout for a little while. I tell my parents that I need to ask Nora a homework question, and I carry a notebook with me to make it more believable.

I ride the elevator downstairs, and check to make sure

nobody is in the hallway or the storage closet before I slip inside.

When I get down to the Hideout, the lights are already on. Oliver is sitting against the wall with the fabric mural. There's a sketchbook on his lap, and he's playing music on his phone.

"Hey, Oliver," I say.

"Hey."

"What are you up to?"

"Drawing some stuff," he says.

"Like what?"

Oliver turns his sketchbook toward me. The page is full of doodles. There's a robot, a skull with a bow on its head, a kid kicking a soccer ball, an owl, and more. It looks like he sketched them out in pencil and is filling them in with black pen.

"Wow, those are really good."

"Thanks. I get in trouble at school sometimes because I can't stop doodling in the edges of my notebook and homework. Even quizzes sometimes. I can't help myself." He laughs.

"If your teachers don't appreciate your art, that's their problem," I say.

"I wish my parents felt that way. They hate all my

doodling, too. But I can come down here and draw, and nobody cares."

"Did you draw any of the stuff that's on the walls?" I ask.

"Some of it."

"You're really talented," I say.

His cheeks turn red.

"Maybe you can teach me how to draw sometime," I say. "I'm terrible."

He grins. "Sure." Then he looks at his phone. "But I should head back upstairs now. I told my parents I went over to Miles's, and it's been a while."

"Oh, okay." I wish he wasn't leaving so soon. Even though I came down here to be alone.

Oliver closes his sketchbook, turns the music off on his phone, and stands up. "See ya."

"Bye."

With Oliver gone and the music off, it suddenly feels eerie down here. This is my first time down here all by myself. Suddenly, I panic that I'm locked in, that Oliver forgot that I was still here when he left and locked the door from the outside. I run up the stairs to check, but the door still opens. *Phew.*

I take my phone out of my pocket and turn on the movie score from *Pirates of the Caribbean.* At first, I walk around the room, waving my arms as if I'm carrying a baton—like the conductor I saw at the New York Philharmonic concert with my mom.

After a while, my arms get tired, so I plop down on one of the beanbag chairs.

I stare at the walls, at all of the drawings and doodles. I think about writing something of my own on the wall. But what? I keep thinking and staring, and then I notice something new. There are a few lines of writing in block letters right below the doodle of the apartment building that I noticed the other day. I'm certain it wasn't there before. It's even in a different color than the other doodles and text around it—it's pale blue while the other doodles around it are mostly in black, with some red and purple. The writing is small, so I lean in closer to read it.

I'M TIRED OF SMILING
WHEN ACTUALLY I'M FALLING APART
I'M TIRED OF HIDING
THE PAIN THAT'S INSIDE MY HEART

Whoa.

That is . . . intense. I read it again. Whoever wrote this sounds like they're hurting a lot. And the thing is, I can relate.

Who could've written this? Only a handful of people in this building know about the Hideout—Nora, plus the other kids I met at the bus stop. And maybe there are more kids that I haven't met yet.

Oliver was just down here. What if it was him? But he was sitting on the other side of the room, and he was using a black marker in his sketchbook.

Am I sure that the poem wasn't here last time? Maybe it's an old message, and this person doesn't even live here anymore.

But deep down, I know it's new. I'm pretty sure I would've noticed it and read it last time I was here. That space was definitely blank before.

That means whoever wrote it lives in this building and is feeling this way right now.

I go to the bin of markers on the bookshelf and grab a green one. Under the poem, I write:

I know exactly how you feel. You are not alone.
Can I help?
~Joy

I have no idea if whoever wrote this message will see my response, but I hope they will. It makes me feel a little better about my own problems to think that my note might make someone hurt a little less.

Maybe we can help each other.

My parents are going to wonder where I am, so I turn off the lights and head back upstairs, feeling slightly less alone. There's someone else in this building dealing with something hard.

It's not just me.

Chapter Thirteen

The next morning, I rush to get ready for school so I can go down to the Hideout before walking to the bus stop. I want to check to see if whoever wrote that poem responded to my message.

Nothing new is written on the wall. I guess that makes sense, since I only wrote my message last night. I decide to keep checking until a new message appears.

Every time I go down to the Hideout, I keep hoping the mysterious poet will be there. I imagine finding them sitting on the beanbag chair, reading my reply, or in the middle of writing back to me. Then we could spill our problems to each other in person and talk until we felt a little better about everything.

None of this happens. Each morning, I'm the only one in the Hideout and there are no new messages. And each morning, I walk to the bus disappointed. I stare at the other kids from the building, wondering which one of them it could be.

Who seems like they're struggling with something? I have no idea. This is only the second week that I'm taking the bus with the other building kids. On Wednesday, when I get to the bus stop, the kids are talking about a Hideout game night—in low voices, so nobody else overhears. I half pay attention as they make plans.

"Want to do it on Friday night?" Miles asks. "We can do what we did the last time—tell our parents we're at different people's apartments."

"Okay!" Elena says. "Now let's talk snacks."

Whoever wrote the poem said they are tired of hiding their true feelings. So whoever it is, they're good at pretending to be happy.

"I can bake cookies," Nora says. "Does everyone like peanut butter blossoms?"

"I'm allergic to peanuts," Oliver says.

"Oh, right," Nora says. "Forgot about that. How about chocolate chip?"

"Works for me," Oliver says.

"I'll bring popcorn," Miles says.

Maybe it's one of the other kids in the building. Nora said that no younger kids go into the Hideout, but what about the high school kids?

Also, there could be other kids in the building that don't take the bus to school. I wish there were a directory somewhere of all of the kids in the building. Maybe Carlos has something like that. But how would I ask him without it being weird?

"Joy?"

I look up to find the others staring at me.

My face gets hot. "Sorry. What?"

"Game night Friday night," Elena says. "Are you in?"

"Oh. Yeah. Definitely."

"Yay!" Nora says. "You can tell your parents you're going to my place, and I'll tell my dad that I'm going to yours."

"Okay." This is actually perfect. The game night will give me the chance to get to know the other kids better and figure out who could've written the poem. "By the way, are there any other kids in the building that go to the Hideout? Besides us? Like, do the older kids go down there?"

"My brothers used to," Elena says. "But once I found out about it, they eventually stopped. I think the older

94

kids got bored with it after a while. Plus, they can drive places and hang out outside the building."

"Yeah, it's really just us," Nora says. "The Fabulous Five. Now that you're here."

"The Fierce Five," Elena says.

"The Fantastic Five," Miles says.

"The Funny Five?" Oliver says with a laugh.

"All of the above," I say out loud, but inside I'm still trying to figure it out. *Which one of you wrote that poem?*

By Friday morning, I'm pretty sure I'll never get a response from the mysterious poet. Whoever they are, it seems pretty clear that they aren't going to write me back. I keep checking, though, in case.

But when I get down to the Hideout this time, I see something new on the wall. I notice it even before I get up close, because the words are in a different color marker. Right underneath my message, in purple ink, are two sentences in the same block letters:

THANKS. IT HELPS TO KNOW SOMEONE ELSE CARES. I'M TIRED OF BEING SAD.
ARE YOU GOING THROUGH SOMETHING TOO?

They wrote back! I almost scream with happiness. This is amazing. I wonder when they wrote this. It must've been last night, unless whoever it is wakes up early. I'm disappointed that I wasn't here to see them.

What do I write next? I grab an orange marker and uncap and recap it a few times while I think. Finally I come up with something.

Yeah. Sometimes I feel like someone took a slingshot and shot me high into the air, and now I'm waving my arms and trying to find a soft place to land. You know?

I exhale as I recap the marker and put it away. It felt good to write that.

Then I uncap the marker and write one more thing.

By the way, who am I talking to? ~Joy

I hope they write me back again—sooner this time.

By Friday afternoon, Nora and I have our Ziggy walking routine down. I pick up Ziggy from Mae's apartment and meet Nora in the lobby. The three of us walk to the park and make the same loop around it. Ziggy seems to have his favorite places to sniff and pee—plus poop. Speaking of that, Nora and I keep our promise to switch off picking it up.

"This job has been a piece of cake, don't you think?" I ask Nora. Ziggy trots a few steps ahead of us.

"Yeah. Super easy," Nora says. "By the end of the summer, I might be able to convince my dad to let me have my own dog."

"I can't wait until we get our first payment tomorrow." I already have a manila envelope ready to store my earnings in. I wrote "piano savings" in big letters on the outside of it.

"I can't wait either." Nora pauses and then says, "You know, there are other dogs in the building."

"I saw one in the lobby the other day. I think it was a lab mixed with some other breed."

"I wonder if any of the other owners would pay for a dog walker."

"Maybe," I say.

"Maybe they'd pay us," Nora says.

"You think?"

"Mae's trusting us to do it, so why not? Both of us have stuff we're saving up for. What if we walk some more dogs at the same time as Zig? Could you hold a second leash?"

"Probably," I say.

"I could definitely hold two leashes. If we got three other dogs at the same rate, then we could each make three times as much. Eighty dollars per week for each of us."

With eighty dollars a week, I might have enough for lessons and a keyboard by the time I start seventh grade this September.

"You're a genius." I grin. "Let's do it. Now how can we get other dog owners to agree to let us walk their dogs?"

"We'll advertise," Nora says. "Put up flyers around the building. But first, we should come up with a good name for a dog-walking business."

"Hmm."

"Joy and Nora Dog-Walking Company," Nora suggests.

"Straight to the point. I like it." I laugh. "But maybe we can come up with something shorter and punchier."

"How about . . ." She pauses and then says, "Joyful Dog Walkers."

My eyes light up. "I love that. But it doesn't have your name in it."

"That's okay. Your name fits better."

"Are you sure?" I ask.

"I'm sure."

"Okay! We have to get our parents' permission first," I say. "Should we put together another list of reasons why they should say yes?"

Nora's mouth twists as she thinks. "We might not

need to. If we wait another week to ask them, then they might be fine with it because they'll see how well we've done with Zig."

"So we'll ask in a week."

"Sounds like a plan," Nora says, and we grin at each other.

"Hey, Ziggy?" I ask, and he turns around at the sound of his name. "What do you think of having other friends with us on your walk?"

He tilts his head to the side like he is thinking about it.

Nora crouches down, and I do the same. "Does that sound like a good idea, Zig?" she asks.

Ziggy comes over to us and licks Nora's face, and then mine.

I giggle. "We'll take that as a yes."

Chapter Fourteen

Having a game night in a secret location means a lot more planning and strategy than meeting up in someone's basement. Getting all of us and our supplies to the Hideout, without anybody else in the building noticing, is almost like a game in itself. We have to be extra sneaky.

The first challenge is getting us all into the storage closet without being seen. If someone saw all five of us walk into the closet together, they'd know something was up. They'd probably go poking around, and it'd only be a matter of time before they found the hidden door to the Hideout. You have to pass the closet to get to the laundry room, and people in this building do laundry at all hours.

So we go down in shifts, starting with Nora and me. When I get down there, Nora is already inside, and she has a backpack with her.

"Yay, you're here," Nora says.

"I'm so excited. Are those the cookies?" I point to her backpack.

She nods. "I made them right before dinner. I had to come up with a reason why I was bringing all of them to your house, so I told Dad and Izzy that I promised I'd give you a whole container. Anyway, let's head downstairs before someone in the hall hears us."

"Right." I brought a backpack, too, and I shift it on my back as Nora opens the Hideout door. I packed a bag of sour cream and onion chips that I found in our kitchen cabinet, an outdoor blanket for all of us to sit on, and a pack of playing cards.

When we get downstairs, Nora turns on the Christmas lights and takes out her cookies. Meanwhile, I go straight to the corner to see if a new message is there.

There is! Under my last note, it says:

I GET WHAT YOU MEAN. COULD THE HIDEOUT BE YOUR SOFT PLACE? IT FEELS LIKE MINE.

I JUST WISH IT COULD FIX MY PROBLEMS.

I notice that they didn't answer my question about who they are. I wonder why.

"Hey, Nora, come over here."

"What?"

"I want to show you something," I say.

Nora comes over, and I point to the last message in the chain. "Do you recognize this handwriting?" Then I point to the poem. "Or this?"

She studies the handwriting and says, "I don't think so."

"I've been writing back and forth with this person," I explain. "This poem was the first message. I could tell they were sad, so I wrote back. I'm dying to know who it is, though. Any ideas?"

"No clue."

"It's not you, is it?" I mean it as a joke, but then I wonder—what if it is Nora? But we talk to each other every day. I think I'd know if she was struggling with anything. I've been telling her about my parents fighting, so I'm pretty sure she'd tell me if something was wrong.

But still, I stare at her extra closely while she answers.

"Me?" she asks. "Are you serious?"

"I'm kidding." I laugh. "But I wish I knew who it was."

She shrugs. "If they didn't say, they probably don't want you to know."

"Yeah, maybe. Anyway, I guess we should finish

setting up." I want to write another note to this mysterious person, but it can wait until later. Maybe during this game night, I can figure out who may have written the note. The first thing I did when I came down here was look to see if there was a response. Maybe that's what the mysterious poet will do, too.

I lay out my blanket in the middle of the room, and a minute later, we hear the Hideout door open. Elena walks down the stairs.

I pay attention to where Elena looks. If she glances at the corner with the messages, then maybe that will tell me something.

But she only looks at us with a huge smile and says, "I have tons of snacks! I raided our cabinets. Plus side to having two older brothers. My parents won't even notice that I took them. They'll think Ethan or Elliot ate them." She gives an evil-sounding laugh.

"Nice!" Nora says.

"Ethan, Elliot, and Elena," I say. "Your parents must like the letter 'E.'"

"I know, right? My brothers are twins, so they wanted their names to go together. And then they kept it going when I was born."

"What grade are they in?" I ask.

"They're juniors in high school. Only one more year

till they're off to college! I can't wait."

"Why, do you have to share a room with them?" I ask.

"Eww, no way." She grimaces. "Their room is the grossest place on the planet. It smells like stinky socks and sweaty soccer uniforms every time I pass by it. Thank goodness our apartment has three bedrooms, so they share a room, and I have my own."

"Your own room," Nora says dreamily. "I'm so jealous. I haven't had my own room since I was three. And I don't even remember it."

"I had my own room until we moved here," I say. "I miss it."

"What game should we play first?" Nora asks, changing the subject. "Twister?" She holds up the box.

"No offense," Elena says. "But I don't want to end up with one of the boys' butts in my face."

Nora cracks up. "Good point. How about Taboo? That's always fun."

The Hideout door opens and closes again, and two sets of footsteps come down the stairs.

"The Fearless Five, together again!" Miles says.

Oliver follows behind with a shy smile on his face.

"I hope one of you brought drinks," Nora says. "We have a lot of snacks, but nothing liquid."

"I thought of that," Oliver says. He turns his backpack

over and a bunch of juice packs fall out. "My mom went to Costco the other day and got a huge box of these."

"Yes!" Nora says. "My dad never lets me have juice."

"What do we do when we have to pee?" I ask.

"Well," Miles says, coming up next to me. "There's this invention called a toilet." His face is totally serious at first, but then he cracks and starts laughing.

I lightly elbow him. "I *mean*, there's no bathroom down here. Do we have to go all the way back to our apartments?"

"There's a bathroom upstairs at the end of the hall. Next to the laundry room," Oliver says. "You can sneak up there when you have to go."

"Thank you, Oliver," I say.

"We have to make sure we clean all of this up when we're done," Elena says. "No crumbs left behind. The last thing we need is a mouse infestation down here."

"Aww, but if there's a mouse, it could be our Hideout pet!" Nora says. "We can name it Squeaker. Or Stuart! Like from the book. That would be *so* cute."

Elena practically gags. "You're joking, right? One time, a mouse found its way inside our cabin at camp, and I almost peed in my pants and *died*."

Nora laughs. "Let's start playing something. Elena already voted against Twister."

Oliver goes over to the corner—*the* corner—and my eyes get wide. Is Oliver who I've been writing to? Is he going over there to check the messages? It would make sense, since he likes doodling on the walls. Maybe he decided to write that poem, too.

But then he picks up the beanbag chairs and brings them over to the blanket. He sits on one of them and grabs a juice pouch.

My shoulders slump. But then I remember why I'm down here—to play games with my new friends. To get to know them better. Not to figure out who's writing the messages. Well, not *just* that.

Solving this mystery will have to wait another day.

I quickly forget about the messages as we play a round of Taboo and then a round of Uno. We can't stop laughing throughout. Elena and Miles are really competitive, and the rest of us have to keep shushing them when they get too loud, so nobody upstairs hears us.

"How is it that no adults know about the Hideout?" I ask during a snack break. I take a bite of Nora's cookie and wash it down with a gulp of juice. "Like, nobody else has noticed the door in the back of the closet before?"

"Probably 'cause there's so much junk back there," Oliver says before stuffing a handful of chips into his mouth.

"People don't notice all sorts of things. Especially adults," Elena says. "This one time, I was on vacation with my family at a beach in Delaware. We stayed in a rental house, and there was this loose floorboard under the window. I noticed because I stepped on it and it shifted. Anyway, when I lifted it up, there were teeth inside. Like four teeth still attached to the gums."

"You're lying," Miles says, wincing.

"I'm not!" Elena says. "I think they were fake teeth, but I wasn't about to get closer to check."

"Gross!" Nora and I say at the same time.

"It was disgusting. My brothers thought it was hilarious and took a bunch of pictures to send to their friends. But seriously, how did the owner not know teeth were there?"

We all shrug and get quiet.

"I'm glad this place is still our secret," Oliver says.

"Same," Elena says.

"For real," Miles says. "I don't know what I'd do if I couldn't come down here to de-stress with you guys."

"Totally," Nora says.

I nod. I'm so glad I have the Hideout now, too, and these four friends.

Chapter Fifteen

As soon as I wake up the next day, I'm ready to go back down to the Hideout to respond to the latest message on the wall. I didn't want to write back when the other kids were around. I know the messages are right there on the wall for anyone to see, but I don't think anyone else is reading them. Tucked away in the corner of the room, they're like a private conversation between me and this mystery person.

Before I can check the Hideout again, Nora and I have to take Ziggy for his Saturday morning walk. Nora meets me at Mae's apartment this time because it's our first pay day. It's my very first pay day *ever*!

"Here you go, girls." Mae hands each of us a crisp twenty-dollar bill.

"Thank you," we say at the same time.

"No, thank *you*," Mae says. "Ziggy's so much happier when he can take a long walk. I really appreciate your help."

Nora grins as she folds up the money and stuffs it into her jeans pocket. While Mae gets Ziggy's leash on, I tell them I'll be right back.

I hurry next door and into my bedroom. My "piano savings" manila envelope is on top of my desk. I stare at the money for a second, feeling proud. I earned this, and soon I'll be able to buy a keyboard and pay for piano lessons all on my own. Once the money's inside, I stick the envelope in the back of my desk drawer for safekeeping.

When Nora and I get back from Ziggy's walk, I tell her that I need to check something in the Hideout. Since I'm normally the one who drops Ziggy off, I take him with me.

"You have to be quiet," I warn him as I carry him into the storage closet.

Nobody else is in the Hideout. I sit on a beanbag chair while Ziggy explores the room, smelling everything, and read the latest message again.

I GET WHAT YOU MEAN. COULD THE HIDEOUT BE YOUR SOFT PLACE? IT FEELS LIKE MINE.

I JUST WISH IT COULD FIX MY PROBLEMS.

How should I respond? I want to know who this person is, but they don't seem to want to tell me yet. If I knew who they were, then maybe I could do more to help them. Maybe we could help each other.

What I really need is to find out more details about this person, so I can figure out who it is. If I'm going to get to the bottom of this, I need to act like a detective.

I think about it some more, and finally grab a marker to write.

Thank goodness for the Hideout.

It may not fix all of your problems, but you know what helps? Dance parties. Also, doing stuff you love. What are you into? ~Joy

I decide to leave it at that. Maybe their answer will be the clue I need to figure out which one of the "Fabulous Five" is writing to me.

"Let's get you home," I tell Ziggy.

Back upstairs, Mom is in the living room dragging the couch away from the wall. Dad is standing there, watching her with a doubtful expression on his face.

"What are you doing?" I ask.

"Rearranging the furniture," Mom says. "We can come up with a better setup in here. Maximize what little space we have."

"It was fine the way it was," Dad says.

"We'll see when I'm done."

"Well, one of Spencer's guys called out, so I'm going to go help him with a project at a client's house," Dad says. "He's going to pick me up and pay me. Is that okay with you?"

"Why wouldn't it be okay with me?" Mom asks. She picks up our armchair that's sitting in the corner of the room. Dad goes over and grabs it from her.

"Over there, please." Mom points to the opposite corner of the room, and Dad puts the chair down. "Thanks."

"I know you don't want me working with Spencer," Dad says.

"That's not what I said," Mom says. "You're twisting my words again."

I wish they would stop bickering about everything. It makes me more and more uneasy, like I'm standing on shaky ground that could collapse at any minute. At least this isn't a full-on argument. Yet. Before it turns into one, I leave the living room.

Malia is in our room changing into her ballet outfit. I glance at my pile of piano books that have been collecting dust since we got here, and I wish I had a lesson today. I grab the book on top and open to a song I was working on with my teacher, Ms. Nancy, before I had to stop my lessons.

I sit at my desk and hum the song, moving my fingers as though the top of my desk were the keys. Maybe I can print out a picture of a keyboard and practice that way. Then I remember that one of my books is a piano theory workbook for practicing, recognizing, and writing the notes on sheet music. I don't need a piano for that, so I quickly come up with a new plan. I'll do at least one exercise in this workbook every single day. By the time I get back to my piano lessons, Ms. Nancy will be impressed by how well I can read music.

I start working on one of the workbook exercises, and then Mom pokes her head into our room.

"Ready to go to ballet, Malia?"

"Yup," Malia says. "See ya later, alligator," she says to me.

"In a while, crocodile," I say back.

"Your dad's going to stay until I get back," Mom tells me. "Then he's going to go help Uncle Spencer."

"Okay."

She leaves, and I finish up the workbook exercise. I'm about to start the next one, but I decide to open the Notes app on my phone instead. On the top, I type "Hideout Messages" and 🕵️ 🤨. Below that, I list everyone I know that could've written them.

Oliver. He'd said that his parents don't like how much time he spends drawing. Maybe it's taking an even bigger toll on him.

Elena. She seems pretty happy, but maybe things aren't so great at home. She has her own room, but that doesn't mean she isn't struggling with something else. At the bus stop, her twin brothers don't pay any attention to her. She doesn't seem to mind, but maybe deep down she really does?

Miles. He likes to make jokes, but what if that's all a cover-up for whatever struggles he's going through?

And then there's Nora. But she said it wasn't her. I don't see why she'd lie to me, not when we're becoming better friends.

Finally, there are the other, older kids in the building. Elena said they don't go down to the Hideout anymore, according to her brothers, but what if that isn't true? What if one of them is still going down there when nobody else is around? Like, late at night or something, when nobody else would see them. Could I be writing to one of the older kids?

All I know is I'm making a connection with whoever it is. And I want to do more to help than write back on the wall.

I stare at the list, turning all of the possibilities around in my head. But I know I won't get an answer just by thinking.

I need to *do* something.

But what?

"Can you help me with something?" I ask Nora a couple of days later while we're walking Ziggy. It's raining out, but only lightly. We're all wearing rain jackets, including Ziggy, who has a bright yellow doggy coat on. It even has a hood. I almost died of cuteness when Mae opened the door and I first saw him wearing it.

Nora and I are also carrying umbrellas. I'm wearing rain boots, and she has on a pair of flowery Doc Martens.

"Help you with what?" Nora asks. "If it's math home-work, you should ask someone else. I'm actually not that bad at it, but I despise it and don't want to look at any more of it than I have to."

We reach a shallow puddle in a dip in the sidewalk,

and Ziggy sniffs at it but then stands there.

"It's just a little water, Ziggy," I say. "You can walk through."

He looks up at us and then back at the puddle, like *no way*.

Nora lifts him up, walks through the puddle, and then places him back on the sidewalk. He licks her hand as thanks.

When we reach the park entrance, Nora passes me the leash, since we usually switch off at this point.

"No math," I say. "Remember those messages I showed you on the Hideout wall on game night—the mysterious person I'm writing to? I want to find out who it is."

"I already told you I don't recognize the handwriting," Nora says, sounding a little annoyed to be repeating herself.

"I know. I was thinking you could help me figure out who it is. We could work together. Two brains are better than one, right? I'll be Sherlock and you'll be . . . what's his sidekick's name?"

"Watson," Nora says.

"Right, Watson," I say. "You'll be Watson."

"First of all, I'm nobody's sidekick," Nora says as she hops over a larger puddle. I lead Ziggy around it. "I'm the hero of my own story."

"You know what I mean!" I say. "C'mon, it could be fun. We're already starting a dog-walking business together. Why not solve a mystery together, too? Maybe that could be our thing. We could call ourselves the Dog-Walking Detectives."

Nora stops walking and looks at me. "You know, that sounds like an awesome movie idea." Her eyes light up. "I'm going to write that down in my idea notebook when I get home."

"You're welcome," I say with a laugh.

It starts raining a little harder, and Ziggy starts whining.

"Maybe we should head back," I say.

Nora agrees, and we turn back toward the park entrance.

"Why do you want to know who's writing the messages so badly, anyway?" Nora asks.

"I guess I relate to them. You know, with all the stuff going on with my parents."

"How *are* things going with your parents?" Nora asks.

"They're still fighting. A lot," I say. "I didn't tell you when it first happened, but my dad even slept at my uncle's house one night. To get some 'space,' my mom said. He never slept away from home when we were living at our house, not unless he was traveling or something."

"Wow. I'm sorry."

"Thanks. I'm scared of what will happen if they can't stop arguing." I shrug. "I don't know, I guess I want to know who this other person is, because it helps me to know I'm not alone in going through something. And I want to help this person."

"What could you do to help them?" Nora asks.

I'm not sure how to answer her. How *could* I help, other than listen to them? And I guess I'm already doing that by reading their messages.

"I don't know," I finally admit. "I'll figure something out. But I'm putting myself in their position. Why write that poem on the wall if you don't want someone to reach out and help? They could've written it in their notebook, or somewhere else private. But they chose to write it in the Hideout, where someone could find it. That must mean something. They want to be found out."

"But what if they *don't* want to be found out?" Nora asks.

"I thought of that. But it's probably Elena, Miles, or Oliver. If they're hurting, don't you want to know so you can help?"

"It could be one of them," Nora says. "Or it could be someone else. We don't know if one of the older kids goes to the Hideout when we're not around."

"True," I say.

We're both quiet for a few moments as we walk, the rain making pitter-patter sounds against our umbrellas, and our shoes squeaking on the wet sidewalk.

Then Nora says, "Okay."

"Okay, as in you'll help me?" I ask.

"I guess I can help," she says. "But I'm not going to be your sidekick. I'll be your . . . advisor. Like Alfred was for Batman."

I laugh. "Deal. And if you do write a Dog-Walking Detective movie, I want some of the credit."

"Well, yeah. And obviously, you're going to compose the score."

"Sounds like a plan." We grin at each other in the rain—until we hear more of Ziggy's whimpers.

"We're going, Zig," Nora says as the rain picks up. "You're the boss."

She scoops him up, and we run home, getting soaked but laughing the whole way.

Chapter Sixteen

I keep checking the Hideout for new messages every morning, but days later, there's still nothing new. Maybe I should've written something else. Or maybe Nora is right, and the person doesn't want to be found. But I have to go with my gut, and my gut says to keep trying.

I grab a marker and write a new message under my last one.

Is everything okay? Hope you're feeling better! Write back soon. ~Joy

Next to that, I draw a picture of a sun with a smiley face. If nothing else, I hope it makes whoever's writing these messages smile.

On Friday, I wake up with extra energy. Today is the day that Nora and I agreed to ask our parents for permission to walk more dogs. I decide to ask Mom and Dad first thing in the morning, before Dad has to drop Mom off at the train station.

I quickly get dressed for school and find both of my parents in the kitchen. Dad is pouring coffee from the pot into two travel mugs—one for him and one for Mom. Mom is taking the creamer out of the fridge. Neither of them are talking, but at least they aren't fighting.

"I need to ask you something," I say. "Both of you."

"Sure, but make it quick," Mom says. "I have to leave for work in a minute. I'm catching an earlier train today."

"Basically, Nora and I want to walk more dogs. Four dogs total, which means two leashes for me to hold, and two leashes for Nora to hold. We've been walking Ziggy for two weeks, and it's going great. Once you get the hang of walking one dog, it's not that hard to hold one more leash. And then we can make more money to put toward our goals. Like my piano lessons. So do I have your permission?"

Mom and Dad look at each other. And then Mom looks

at her watch. "Ahh, I really need to leave. Can we talk about this later?"

"Say yes now!" I say. "Please? I promise we can handle it. We've thought this through."

"Uh." Mom's mouth twists as she looks at Dad. "How about we talk about it in the car and then Dad will tell you our answer when he gets back." She comes over to me and kisses my forehead. Then she leaves the kitchen saying, "Malia, come say bye-bye."

I wait for Dad to come back from dropping off Mom. As soon as he walks in the door, I say, "Can I do it? I heard you tell Mae that working for yourself is the way to go. Nora and I would be opening our own dog-walking business. You could even help us! You know, since you're working with Uncle Spencer more and more, you can give us business tips."

Dad's expression shifts to curiosity.

I've got him, I think, though I don't dare smile yet.

"Mae did say yesterday that she's really happy with you two walking Ziggy," Dad says.

Thank you, Mae, I think.

"If you think you can handle walking two dogs each, then we can give it a try," Dad says. "Mom agrees. But we'll start with a trial period. If it gets too hard to keep that many dogs under control, you'll have to stop."

"Thanks, Dad!" I go over and hug him.

"You're welcome. My little entrepreneur," Dad says as he hugs me back. "It must run in the family. I can't wait to tell Spencer about this."

I smile.

"Oh, and I have good news," Dad says. "I got an email from one of the jobs I applied for. I have an in-person interview next week. Guess I should go ahead and shave." He rubs his beard, which is still growing in.

"That's amazing!" I hug him again, squeezing harder this time.

"Hopefully it goes well. I like the sound of the company."

"You'll do great, Dad." I grin.

Finally, things are looking up.

Nora gets the okay from her dad, too, so after school, we get together to research how to start a dog-walking business. We also begin designing our flyers. On one website, we find a list of supplies every dog walker should own: a spare leash, lots of baggies, and a reusable water bottle and plastic bowl to keep the dogs hydrated. We already have some of those supplies for Ziggy, but we'll need more. We decide to use some of our first two weeks of earnings from Mae to pay for these supplies.

"You know what I just thought of?" Nora asks as we're picking out items online. Her dad agreed to let us use his credit card to place the order, and we'll pay him back.

"What?" I ask.

"Walking four dogs means picking up four times the amount of poop." She wrinkles her nose.

I laugh. "I know, so gross. But it'll be worth it for eighty bucks a week."

Over the weekend, we print our flyers out and hang them up around the building. We put them in each stair-well on each floor, plus inside the elevators. We also slip them under the doors of the tenants that Nora says own dogs. Nora's knowledge of where everyone lives in the building pays off big-time.

We create an email address for our company and put it on the flyers. We also include a picture of the two of us walking Ziggy. Nora says that everyone in the building knows Mae and Ziggy, so if they see that Mae has trusted us with walking Ziggy, they should trust us with their dogs, too.

I check our company email address whenever I can, to see if anyone has sent us a message. On Tuesday night, there's finally a new email waiting for us.

Hi, Joy and Nora,

I saw the flyer for your dog-walking business. We'd love our dog, Tank, to get an extra walk each day during the week. Can you let us know when you're available to chat more? Thank you!

Best,

Rebecca and Noah Wilkinson

Apartment 4E

I immediately text Nora.

JOY: OMG check our email. We have a potential client!

A few seconds later, Nora texts back.

NORA: OMG YAY! 🎉 🎉 🐶 🐶

I email the Wilkinsons back, and Rebecca agrees to interview us after she gets home from work the following day.

"Have you met Tank already?" I ask Nora when it's time to head to Rebecca and Noah's apartment for our interview. "I wonder what kind of dog he is. I bet he's big and strong. I hope we can handle him."

"I've seen him before." Nora gives a sly smile. "He

definitely lives up to his name. You'll see."

When we get to the fourth floor, we knock on the door for 4E. I hear some barking, but it isn't that loud.

The door opens.

"Hi, I'm Rebecca," the woman on the other side says. She's holding a dog—a pretty small dog. He barks again. His dark eyes are really expressive, and he stares at us like he's trying to size us up.

I look at Nora, who's smiling at me. "See?"

"This is Tank," Rebecca says. "He's a little guy, but he has a big personality."

"Hi, Tank," I say. "What kind of dog is he?"

"A mini pinscher."

Tank is around the same height as Ziggy, but a lot leaner. He has a shiny black coat with some brown areas around his face and legs. His ears point up.

"He's so cute," Nora says.

"Yeah, he's adorable," I say.

"Why don't we take him outside?" Rebecca asks. "We can do your interview out there."

"Sure," Nora says.

Rebecca puts a harness on Tank that has a leash attached to it. She hands the leash handle over to me, and we head to the elevator.

When we get outside to the patch of grass in front of

the building, Tank immediately starts doing his business.

"He's pretty efficient," Rebecca says, with a laugh. "So, when you girls walk dogs, do you make sure to clean up after them?"

"Always," Nora says. "We ordered a whole bunch of poop bags." She pats the pocket of her denim jacket, where she's stored a couple of them.

Rebecca nods. "Great. And where do you plan to walk?"

"Around the park behind the building," I say. "We take Ziggy there, and he loves it."

"Go ahead and walk a little bit, so I can see you two in action," Rebecca says.

"Okay," Nora says.

"I'll walk a few steps behind," Rebecca says.

Nora and I walk ahead with Tank, and suddenly I'm nervous with Rebecca watching us. Walking dogs is so easy, but this is the first time we've had an audience.

Tank seems a little wary of us as well. He keeps looking back to make sure Rebecca is still here.

When it's time to cross the street, I look both ways extra carefully before walking across.

Once we're inside the park, Tank seems happier. When we pass under a tree with some birds chirping inside,

Tank starts barking up at them. It's pretty funny.

The rest of the walk goes smoothly. But Nora and I don't talk much, like we normally do when we're walking Ziggy, since Rebecca is right behind us. I'm glad that Rebecca won't be following us every time we walk her dog.

When we get back to the front of our building, I hand Tank's leash back to Rebecca.

"You guys did a great job. I'd love to hire you to walk him in the afternoons during the week. Starting Monday, if that's okay."

"More than okay," I say, toning down my excitement so I sound professional.

"The thing is, we're at work until six every day, but you've been walking Ziggy earlier than that, right?"

"Yes," Nora says.

"I've been wondering about how you could pick up and drop off Tank when we're not home," Rebecca says.

I hadn't thought of that. If the Wilkinsons aren't home, then how will we get Tank? Mae is always home when I need to get Ziggy.

"We have a plan for that," Nora says.

I look over at her. *What plan?*

Nora continues. "Since Carlos has the keys to everyone's

apartment, for when he has to do maintenance or whatever, would you be okay with him letting us into your apartment when it's time to get Tank? That way, we won't need our own key."

Carlos, the building's super! It's the perfect solution. I grin at Nora, who smiles back.

"That's a good idea," Rebecca says. "Yes, I think that could work."

"Okay, we can go over and talk to Carlos now, and make sure he's okay with it," Nora says.

"Great. Once you talk to him, can you ask him to give me a call?" Rebecca asks.

"Will do," Nora says.

"Perfect. Thanks again. Tank seemed to enjoy his walk with you."

"We did too." I lean over and rub the top of Tank's head. He wags his stubby tail and licks my hand. Guess he likes me now. "See you later, Tank."

Rebecca gives us one more smile before going inside the building with Tank.

Once she's gone, I nudge Nora. "That was amazing! Why didn't you tell me about the Carlos thing before?"

Nora laughs. "I actually only thought of it in the moment!"

"What? That was quick thinking."

"Seriously," she says. "Now let's go talk to Carlos and make sure he's fine with it."

"Do you think he'll agree to it?" I ask.

Nora tucks her hair behind her ear. "I hope so. Or else we won't get to keep our new client."

Chapter Seventeen

"*Mateo pushed me!*" *a girl's* voice whines from inside Carlos's apartment.

Nora and I stand in the hallway right outside.

"One second," Daniela, Carlos's wife, says to us. She turns away, partially closing her apartment door.

Nora and I shrug at each other.

"Mateo," Daniela says sternly. "What did I say about pushing? Disculpate con tu hermana."

"Sorry, Sofia," Mateo says.

"Gracias, mijo." Daniela turns back to me and Nora. "Sorry about that. You said you're looking for Carlos? He should be in the basement. He's fixing an issue with the trash chute. There's always something in this building."

"Oh, okay," Nora says. "We'll go look for him. Thanks!"

We say goodbye, and then Nora and I take the stairs one floor down to the basement level. I haven't been down here before, but Nora leads us to a room that has the trash chute—and Carlos. He's standing on a small ladder looking up at a big metal tube coming out of the ceiling. Right below the tube is a large container full of smelly garbage bags. This room has a door leading outside, and it's open. But it still smells terrible, so I stop breathing out of my nose and only breathe from my mouth.

I stare at the trash chute. Huh. *So that's how that works.* I've seen my parents go into this little closet on our floor and push our garbage bags through a hole in the wall. But I had no idea what happened to the trash once it went down the chute. Looks like it all lands down here.

In our house, one of my parents would take the trash outside. It was never that many bags. Does Carlos have to take out all of the trash bags for the whole building, all by himself? I think back to what Mae said about not letting people take advantage of you. I hope Carlos gets paid well for all the work he does here.

"Hey, Carlos," Nora says, interrupting my thoughts.

Carlos turns toward us, surprised. "What are you two doing down here?"

"Joy and I want to ask you something," Nora says. "It's about our dog-walking business."

"I saw the flyers," he says. "You two are smart, already making money at your age."

"Well, Rebecca in 4E is letting us walk her dog, Tank," Nora says. "But she wants us to walk him when she's not home. Since you have the key to her apartment, we wanted to know if you could let us into her place when we need to pick up Tank. She's fine with it, and she said you should call her."

Carlos nods. "I'll give her a call when I'm finished down here. If it's okay with Rebecca, then it's fine with me."

"Great!" Nora says. "Thank you so much."

Carlos turns to me. "How are you liking the building so far, Joy?"

I pause, not sure how to answer. I guess it's not that bad, but I still wish I were in my old house. The best part is the Hideout, but I can't tell Carlos that.

"I'm still getting used to it," I say. "But I love being neighbors with Nora."

"Aww, me too!" Nora says.

Carlos smiles at the two of us. "I'm glad to hear it. Well, I'd better get back to work. The trash chute is not going to fix itself."

"Good luck!" Nora says.

We go back upstairs, and I'm happy to be able to breathe out of my nose again. Nora and I say goodbye when the elevator gets to my floor.

At my door, before I can even get my key out, I hear my parents arguing on the other side. I groan, wishing, once again, that I didn't have to go inside.

That weekend, I'm in the laundry room throwing my dirty clothes in one of the washing machines, when Miles walks in, dragging a laundry bag behind him, plus a small container of detergent.

"Hey, Joy."

"Miles. Hey."

"You've got chores, too?" he asks.

"Yup." I pour detergent into the little cup in the machine, close the door, and use the laundry card my parents gave me to turn it on.

"I saw your flyers," Miles says, as he opens one of the other empty washing machines. "You and Nora are walking dogs now?"

"Yeah! At first it was just Ziggy, but now we're going to start walking another dog named Tank. We want to walk four dogs total."

"Nice. And you get paid for walking them?" Miles finishes loading his laundry and turns his machine on. The sounds of multiple machines spinning laundry around fill the room.

"Yeah. I'm trying to save up for piano lessons and a keyboard."

"For real? Do you play?"

"A little," I say. "I started taking lessons in the fall, but my parents said I have to stop them for now. They don't have the money anymore."

"I know what that's like," Miles says.

"Really?"

"Yeah. The school me and Elena go to—it's a private school. But both of us got scholarships. It only covers tuition, though. If we want to join an after-school activity or go on one of the field trips, we have to pay for that separately. My parents aren't poor or anything, but a lot of these other families are rich. Like, rich. My parents can't throw money around like that."

"Wow. Do you even like going to that school?"

He shrugs. "It's fine. My parents want me to go there because they think it'll help me get into a good college.

It has a high school, too."

It seems like there's a "but" coming, so I wait for Miles to keep going.

"But," Miles says, "it sucks being one of the only Black kids there. There are, like, four of us total in the whole middle school."

I give a sympathetic nod. Even though I don't go to his school, I know exactly what he's talking about. The public schools in town are pretty diverse, but there have been plenty of times in my life when I've been the only Black girl in a situation. Most of the time it's fine, but sometimes I can't help but feel . . . different.

Like when we had to go swimming during gym class at my old school. I was the only one who wore a swim cap to help protect my natural hair from the chlorine. My classmates with straight hair didn't have to worry about that, I guess, because they never wore one. It also always took longer for me to get ready after being in the pool, because my darker skin looks a million times better with lotion to keep it from getting ashy. But the girls with lighter skin could skip that step.

"And, like, when I do talk to the other Black kids, sometimes it's like they think I'm too nerdy for them or something," Miles says. "One of them made fun of me for being excited about the last *Star Wars* movie."

"That's ridiculous. Everyone loves *Star Wars*."

"Right," Miles says. "Meanwhile, a bunch of other kids went to Disney World over winter break with their families. They went to Galaxy's Edge and rode all of the *Star Wars* rides. When they got back, they said I had to go, since they know I'm obsessed with the movies. But Disney World is expensive. I didn't say that, though. They don't get it."

"I'm sorry," I say.

"It's okay."

Wait. Could Miles have written the poem because he's struggling with being one of the only Black kids at school? It makes sense. I know how hard it can be.

But how do I find out for sure?

"If you ever, you know, get down about things, you can talk to me," I say.

"Thanks. I'm fine, though. I mean, this stuff sucks, but I've been dealing with it since elementary school. I don't let it get me down. Those guys have nothing better to do than be mean."

Hmm. Maybe Miles is not the one writing me messages. Unless he's this good at hiding his true feelings. But he seems pretty genuine.

"At least I get to hang out with you guys in the Hideout," Miles says. "You all like me the way I am."

"Yeah." I smile. "I definitely won't judge. I'm a *Star Wars* nerd, too."

I pause and then ask, "Do you ever hang out in the Hideout by yourself?"

He shakes his head. "Never. I only go with you guys. Otherwise it's kinda creepy down there. Why?"

"No reason."

"Hey, want to do something fun?" Miles asks.

I'm thrown by the quick change of subject. "Uh, sure. What?"

He goes over to a rolling laundry cart that's in the corner of the room. It basically looks like a rectangle-shaped metal basket with legs and wheels. "Get in," he says.

"You want me to get in that thing?"

"Yup." He rolls a second cart so the two carts are next to each other along the wall. Then he climbs into one of them.

I don't think. I climb into the other cart. Miles holds on to the edge of my cart with one hand and on to the wall with the other.

"On the count of three, we'll both push away from the wall at the same time. Whoever's cart goes the farthest, wins."

I grin. "Got it." I shift positions in the cart so I'm sitting on my knees. I put one hand against the wall behind me and get ready to push.

Miles starts counting. "One . . . two . . . three!"

He pushes himself off as he's saying "three," and meanwhile I was waiting for him to finish saying "three." So by the time I push myself off the wall, he's already rolling across the room.

I push myself off the wall anyway while saying, "Hey! That's not fair. You went too early!"

Miles is laughing as he comes to a stop. "That was completely fair! And anyway, it doesn't matter when you push off. It's the distance you go that matters."

As he's saying that, I come to a stop a couple of feet closer than him. He clearly won that round. "Okay, fine," I say. "Let's do it again."

We have to get out of the carts so we can roll them back to the wall and start over. As we're climbing back into them, an older white man comes into the room. When he notices us sitting in the carts, he gives us a look that instantly shows his disapproval. Then he takes the last empty cart and uses it to transfer his laundry from a washing machine to a dryer. Miles and I are silent. We glance at each other and try not to laugh.

When the man is done transferring his clothes and turning on the dryer, he shoots us one more disapproving look before leaving the room again.

When we hear his footsteps retreat back down the hall, Miles and I look at each other and burst into laughter.

"Did you see his face?" Miles asks between laughs.

"Oh my gosh, thank goodness there was a third cart. Imagine if he had to ask us to use one of ours?"

Miles laughs some more.

"Do you think he'll tell Carlos?" I ask. "I don't want to get in trouble."

"I doubt it. That's Mr. Hollins. He can be grumpy sometimes, but he's harmless. I don't think he'll tell on us."

"So round two then?"

"Yeah!"

We get ourselves back in the starting position, and this time I push myself off the wall at the right moment, and I push harder this time. I end up going farther and win this round.

We play a few more rounds, and by the time I head back upstairs, I've learned two things.

1. Miles is a lot of fun.
2. I'm pretty sure he's not the one writing the messages on the Hideout wall. If he's never down there by himself, when would he have written the notes?

I can cross him off my list. One suspect down, two to go.

Chapter Eighteen

Nora has a huge grin on her face when I meet up with her to walk Ziggy on Sunday morning.

"Guess what?" she asks as soon as I step off the elevator. "We have our last two dog clients! I just ran into Jack and Peter. They're the couple that lives in 3G. They have two dogs—Rollie and Lillie. They're Wheaton terrier siblings, and they're so cute. Jack and Peter asked if we could walk them in the afternoons!"

"Oh wow," I say. "Do we have to do an interview like with Rebecca?"

"I asked, but they said no. Jack and Peter have known me for as long as I've lived here. They used to babysit me sometimes after school. The dogs know me, too, so it should be fine. They said we can start walking them tomorrow."

"Awesome!" I say. "That means we have all four dogs now."

"Yup." Nora gives a satisfied smile. "Joyful Dog Walkers is officially booked."

"Yay!"

Ziggy starts whining and pulling on his leash toward the door leading outside.

"Okay, Ziggy, we're going," I tell him.

We head outside and walk toward the park. It's super bright out, so I lower my sunglasses from the top of my head. Nora's Mets hat blocks the sun from her eyes.

"I have good news, too," I say.

"What is it?" Nora asks.

"I talked to Miles yesterday in the laundry room. I didn't flat-out ask him if he wrote the messages in the Hideout, but I talked to him about other stuff. He's so funny." I laugh, remembering how fun it was to race the laundry carts. I never would've thought to do that. Miles ended up winning the majority of our rounds, but I told him that we have to do a rematch sometime.

"And?" Nora asks.

"I don't think he wrote the messages," I say. "He talked

about some stuff he's going through at school, but he seems to be handling it all okay. Also, he said he's never down in the Hideout by himself."

"Okay . . . ," Nora says. We stop walking while Ziggy pees. "So what will you do now?"

"I need to talk to Elena and Oliver, since it's probably one of them. Which one should I talk to first?"

Nora shrugs. "I don't know."

"That's all you have to say?" I ask. "You're supposed to be my advisor!"

She laughs. "I thought you were joking around."

"I mean, part of it was me being silly," I admit. "But I could use your help, since you know all of the other kids better than I do."

"We need to focus on our dog-walking business," Nora says. "I want to do a good job. I've been researching the camera I'm saving up for, and I really want it."

"Don't worry, this won't get in the way of us walking the dogs."

Nora doesn't say anything else, so we're quiet for a minute while we walk.

"So will you go with me to talk to Elena or Oliver, once I figure out which one to talk to first?" I ask.

"Sure," she says. "If I'm available."

Why wouldn't you be available? I decide not to ask. At this point, I'm more than ready to change the subject. "Let's talk about tomorrow then. After school, I'll drop off my stuff and pick up Ziggy as usual. Then should I meet you at Carlos's apartment so we can get the other dogs?"

Nora perks up. "Sounds good. I'm so excited about this."

"Me too."

I wish Nora was also excited about finding out who wrote the Hideout messages, but there's nothing I can do about that. I guess it makes sense that I'm more invested, since I'm the one who's been writing to this person this whole time.

If Nora can't help me, it'll be fine. I'll have to solve this mystery on my own.

Nora clutches a dog leash in each hand. "I can't believe we're doing this!"

"I know!" I squeal. I hold tight to my two leashes, too. I've got Ziggy's and Rollie's leashes, and Nora has Tank's and Lillie's. Since Rollie and Lillie are twice as big as the other two dogs, Nora and I decided to split them up and each walk one bigger dog and one smaller dog.

Rollie and Lillie have fluffy fur and adorable faces. They're mostly tan, but the fur around their mouths is darker brown. It's almost like they have beards. They were friendly when we picked them up from their owners.

Now, Nora and I are standing in front of our building, ready to take our very first walk with all four dogs.

"Are you nervous?" I ask. "I am, a little. I hope we can handle all four of them."

"I am too," Nora says. "But we've got this."

It's warm in the afternoon sun. On our street, cars are driving by with their windows down and music playing. A few people are jogging or on their bikes. It's a perfect day to walk some dogs.

I'm carrying a backpack that I found in our coat closet, one of my dad's extra ones. I put all of our supplies in it—baggies, dog treats, water bottles, and a plastic bowl in case the dogs get thirsty while we're out.

"Ready, pups?" Nora asks the dogs. Ziggy wags his tail, and Tank jumps up on Nora's leg. Meanwhile, Rollie and Lillie pull our leashes toward the sidewalk.

It takes us longer than usual to get to the park because we keep having to stop so a different dog can pee. At one point, when we reach a fire hydrant, Rollie peeing on it starts a whole domino effect. One after another, all of the other dogs pee on the exact same spot. Tank goes last, and right after that, Rollie goes to pee on it again.

As soon as he's done, I pull him away from the hydrant. "Let's go before they all keep peeing here."

"Maybe we can jog the rest of the way to the park," Nora says. "So they don't get distracted by anything else before we get there."

"Good idea." We start jogging. Right away, the dogs trot next to us. Tank looks like a small galloping horse when he runs.

We slow down once we get to the park's entrance.

"Water break?" I ask. "They're panting. I think that's how they sweat."

"Okay," Nora says.

We walk to a bench and sit down. I loop both leashes on one hand so I can slip my backpack off. I pull out a plastic bowl and pour water into it. When I put it on the ground, all of the dogs try to get to it first.

"One at a time," I say.

They don't listen, but eventually each of them gets a few licks of water.

After Nora takes a gulp from her water bottle, she asks, "Want to hear something cool?"

"Sure."

"Today I told Ms. Francis about how I'm working on a screenplay." Ms. Francis is one of the sixth-grade English teachers. "Turns out she took a couple of screenwriting classes in college, so she knows a little about it. She offered to read my script for me when I'm done!"

"That's awesome!"

"I know, right? Now I really need to finish it. I'm going to work on it every night from now on, after homework. It's already June and we have, what, three weeks of school left? I want to give it to Ms. Francis soon so there's time for her to read it before summer break. Then I can use her notes to fix it over the summer." I can tell how excited Nora is because she starts talking even faster. "And then, if we keep walking dogs and making money, maybe I'll have enough to buy my camera by the time school starts again. I can start filming this fall!"

"You'll get it done in time," I tell her. "It's going to be great."

"Thanks." She beams, but then her expression gets serious. "I need every minute of my free time to work on my script. So I can't help you talk to Elena or Oliver about the Hideout message stuff. Sorry."

"It's okay," I say. "I can talk to them on my own."

"Cool," Nora says. "I'm glad you understand."

"Of course," I say. "That's what friends are for."

Nora leans over and rests her head on my shoulder. "You're the best. Seriously."

I smile and lean my head in.

The rest of our walk goes well. By the time we get back to our building, the dogs have peed several more times, Nora and I have each picked up poop, and Rollie and Lillie have little leaves and twigs stuck to their beard fur from sniffing the ground so much. It's really cute, but Nora and I pull all of it off before we head inside.

We did it. We survived walking four dogs, all by ourselves!

I'm in such a good mood that after dinner, I decide to check the Hideout wall again, to see if there's anything new. It's been over a week since I left my last message telling the mysterious person to write back soon. I haven't checked as much over the last few days because I was starting to think I'd never see another reply.

But when I get to the corner, I notice new words written underneath mine.

You Don't Have To Worry About Me Anymore.

I stare at it and read it a couple more times. What does this mean? Why would they write that?

Something about this message seems . . . ominous. Like there's more to it. Like they might . . . hurt themself.

I have to get to the bottom of this—fast.

Chapter Nineteen

Elena's sitting on a bench outside our building when Nora and I get back from walking the dogs the next day. There's a book open on her lap and a can of soda on the ground.

When she spots us, she says, "Oh my gosh, these dogs! So cute. I can't believe you're walking all of them."

"Hey, E," Nora says. "Yeah, we're official now."

Lillie and Rollie immediately go over to Elena and lick her face. "Aren't you such a good doggie," Elena says in a baby voice as she rubs their heads and chins. "And you too. Such good doggies." They both give satisfied grins.

Meanwhile, Ziggy plops down on the sidewalk,

panting. Tank goes to sniff Elena's soda can, but Nora tugs on his leash to pull him away. Elena picks up the soda can and takes a gulp.

"What're you up to?" I ask as I fill our dog bowl with some more water and place it on the ground in front of Ziggy. He slurps up some water, and after he's done, Tank does the same.

Elena holds up the book—*A Long Walk to Water* by Linda Sue Park. "Homework. My brothers have a friend over, and they're playing video games. They're being so loud, so I came out here. I was going to go"—she lowers her voice—"to *the Hideout*, but since it's so nice out, I decided to sit outside instead."

"It is really nice out," I say. "I should bring my homework out here after we drop the dogs off."

"Okay!" Elena says. "You too, Nora."

"I would," Nora says, "but I want to work on my screenplay before I do my homework. I came up with a good idea for a scene today. During gym, actually."

"Oh, when you're ready to film, can I audition to be in your movie?" Elena asks.

"Sure! From what I saw on the LARP videos you showed me, you'd be great."

Elena grins.

Ziggy starts pulling toward the front door.

"We should probably get the dogs home," I say. "But I'll come back out."

"Okay," Elena says.

Nora and I head inside.

"You sure you don't want to sit outside with us?" I ask Nora after we ring Carlos's doorbell. "I'm gonna talk to Elena about the messages. But you can work on your screenplay."

I didn't bother telling Nora about the last message that I found—*You don't have to worry about me anymore*—since she's made it clear she'd rather focus on other things.

"I'm sure," Nora says. "As soon as I get this screenplay to Ms. Francis, I'll be free to hang out again."

"We should have another game night to celebrate," I say.

"Yeah!"

"Hey, girls," Carlos says as he opens the door.

Ten minutes later, the dogs are all back in their apartments, and I'm back in mine. Dad's cooking dinner—pasta and meat sauce, from the smell of it. My favorite. Malia is sitting at the dining room table doing her homework. Mom's not home from work yet.

"*Daaad*," Malia says as I pass by her on the way to the bathroom. "I need help!"

"One second," Dad says over the sound of the vent fan above the stove.

After I wash all of the dried dog slobber off my hands, I switch my dog-walking backpack for my school backpack in my room.

In the living room, Dad's leaning over Malia, helping her with a math worksheet.

"I'm going to do my homework outside for a little while, with Elena. She's sitting on the bench out front."

"Okay," Dad says. "I'm picking your mom up from the train in forty minutes, so be back for dinner by then."

"Got it."

Outside, Elena is on the same spot of the bench, flipping to the next page in her book.

I sit next to her. "I'm back."

She uses her finger to hold her place in her book. "Hey."

I open my backpack, take out a folder, and flip through it as if I'm figuring out which homework assignment to do first. But I'm actually thinking about how to ask Elena about the Hideout messages, without flat-out asking her about them.

"Do you have to do this a lot?" I ask. "Leave your apartment because your brothers are being too loud or whatever?"

"Sometimes. They can be *really* loud."

I laugh. "Do you get along with them?"

"Yeah. I mean, we don't fight much. We just like different things. What about you? You have a little sister, right?"

"Yeah. We get along fine. She kind of looks up to me."

"That's cute."

"Yeah, it's just hard when I have to be the strong one for her. Like when my parents argue, I tell her that it's going to be okay, even if I don't know that for sure."

Wait. Why did I say that?

"Sorry." I look down at my homework folder. "I didn't mean to get so . . . personal."

"No, that's okay." When I look at Elena again, there's a sympathetic expression on her face. "I'm sorry you're dealing with that."

"Thanks."

"If you ever need someone to vent to, I'm a good listener."

I smile. "Thanks. Same with you . . . if you ever need to talk about anything."

"That's why I love the Hideout. It's nice that we can sneak away and hang out with each other when we need it."

"Yeah."

"Plus, it's always there when I need a break from my family."

"Do you get along with your parents?" I ask.

Elena nods. "I'm the youngest, and the only girl. So I get away with a lot." She laughs.

"Lucky." I pause and then say, "Tell me more about LARP camp. It sounds so interesting."

Elena puts her book down and grins. "I know it's kind of nerdy, but it's so fun. The camp is basically a normal sleepaway camp, except in between swimming in the lake and building campfires, we get into character and play. The counselors do it with us."

She tells me all about her character—a fairy—and how she fits into the world that they're all playing.

"Getting dressed up is the best part. You saw my Renaissance Faire picture."

I remember seeing it on her phone my first time at the bus stop. "You looked amazing. You're meant to be a fairy."

She blushes. "Thanks. I want to start making my own costumes. My mom just got me a sewing machine so I can learn."

"That's really cool." Hearing her talk about LARP reminds me of myself when I talk about movie scores. I love that she's also passionate about something.

We're quiet for a moment as a car pulls into the building driveway and parks in an assigned spot.

"By the way, do you ever draw on the walls in the Hideout?" I ask. "Or write anything on them?"

"No," Elena says. "I'm terrible at drawing. And my handwriting is like chicken scratch. Sometimes when I read notes I took during class, I can't understand what I wrote. It's bad." She laughs.

The handwriting in the messages is pretty neat, I think, picturing them again in my mind. So Elena must not have written them.

The older man that Miles and I saw in the laundry room the other day—Mr. Hollins—gets out of the car that just parked, and he passes by us as he enters the building. He's holding a takeout bag, and I get a whiff of Mexican food. Now I wish Dad was making tacos instead of pasta.

"Oliver draws on the walls sometimes," Elena says. "Have you seen his stuff before? He's amazing."

"Yeah, he's always sketching on the bus to school."

It's got to be Oliver then. He's the only one left. He has to be writing those messages. Unless someone else goes down to the Hideout that I don't know about. I'll have to talk to Oliver next to be sure, but maybe I've solved this mystery. I have to figure out how to ask him about it.

More important, I need to make sure he's okay.

Chapter Twenty

All week, I try to find a moment to talk to Oliver alone, but he's never in the Hideout when I go down there. I don't want to talk to him about this on the bus or at school, while other kids are around, so I decide to visit his apartment on Saturday.

While I'm finishing up my homework so I can forget about it for the weekend, Mom pokes her head into my room. "Hey, honey, can you come into the living room for a minute?"

"Okay." I stick my pencil into my textbook to hold my spot.

When I get into the living room, Malia's already there

on the couch, next to Mom. Dad's sitting on the armchair. Mom moves over, pats the space on the couch between her and Malia, and I sit down.

"We're having a family meeting," Malia says, matter of fact. "Mommy says we can have ice cream after."

Family meeting? The last time we had one, our parents told us that we were selling our house. I switch back and forth between Mom and Dad, trying to figure out if this is good or bad news. Dad's leaning on his knees with his hands clasped in front of him.

"What's going on? Wait, did you hear back about that job?" I ask Dad. "You got it. Is that it?" For a second, I imagine my parents telling me that Dad did get the job, and somehow, we're able to get our house back.

But Dad exhales and shakes his head. "It doesn't look like I'm getting that job."

"Oh," I say. "But you said you nailed the interview."

"I did. I mean, I thought I did. But it was really competitive."

"Did they say why they didn't hire you?"

"No. Actually, they haven't returned my emails or calls, so I don't know for sure. But I'm pretty sure they went with someone else by now. They said they wanted to fill the position quickly."

"But if you don't know for sure, maybe there's still a chance," I say.

"Maybe," Dad says, but he doesn't look all that hopeful.

"If it's not about the job, then what's this all about?" I look over at Mom, who hasn't said a word since I sat down.

She clears her throat. "Girls, I want you to know that your dad and I love you both very much, and this is not your fault at all."

I freeze. "What's . . . not our fault?" Why do I feel like I'm about to be flung into the air by a slingshot again?

"Things have been stressful, with selling the house and the move. Your dad's job search," Mom says. "We've decided that what might help is if your dad spent a little time . . . away . . . from the apartment."

"Away where?" Malia asks.

"Yeah. What does that mean?" I ask.

"I'm going to go stay with Uncle Spencer for a little while," Dad says. "But you're still going to see me every day. Spencer's going to use his work truck and let me borrow his other car. I'll still come over in the mornings to take Malia to school. I'll still pick her up in the afternoons and hang out here with you both until your mom gets home. And we'll still do things together on the weekends."

"Wait, *what?*" I ask. "You're moving out?"

"Only for a little while," Dad says.

"But why?" I ask. "I don't understand."

"I don't want Daddy to live somewhere else." Malia starts crying. Mom gets up and moves Malia to her lap so Malia can hug her.

"We need to work out a few things," Mom says. "We're going to start seeing a counselor. Someone to help us deal with all of the stress I talked about. And in the meantime, your dad and I think that having a little space will help."

Space. It's because this apartment is too small. If we were in the house, Dad wouldn't need to go stay with Uncle Spencer in order to get space. He could hang out in the living room, or his office, or the basement. But because all we can afford right now is this small apartment, now my parents can't stand to be near each other.

What comes after separation? Divorce.

Mom must see the expression on my face, because she suddenly says, "We're not getting a divorce. This is temporary. I promise."

There's that word again. *Temporary.*

So far, none of the changes I've been experiencing lately have been temporary.

My eyes well up with tears, but I don't want Malia to see me cry. I have to be the strong one.

But that's the problem, isn't it? I always have to be the strong one for Malia. I shouldn't have to do that. I'm still a kid, too. Mom and Dad shouldn't put me in this position.

"It's going to be okay," Dad says, reaching over to squeeze my knee. "We're going to be okay."

"I don't believe you." I swallow a sob, which causes a painful lump to form in my throat. The tone of my voice makes Malia stop crying for a minute, and she lifts her head off Mom's shoulder to look at me. "Are you even thinking of me and Malia when you make these decisions? Or are you only thinking about yourselves?"

"I know you're upset, but I don't like your tone," Mom warns.

"Joy—" Dad begins.

"No," I say. "This isn't okay. None of this is okay."

A small hand covers mine. Malia's. "It's okay if you want to cry," she says. It's something I've said to her many times over the last few months.

That does it. I can't hold the sob back anymore. It hurts too much. It bursts out of me, and my chest heaves as I try to get words out.

"Do you . . . understand how hard it is for me? When you're arguing . . . I'm the one who has to comfort Malia and . . . tell her it's going to be okay. I . . . have to hide my feelings . . . for her sake. But now you're . . . moving out?

That's going to make everything . . . worse!"

"Breathe," Dad says, coming to sit next to me. "In and out, like this."

I do what Dad says and calm down a little.

"Let's talk about this," Mom says.

"Was this your idea?" I ask her. "Are you making Dad leave?"

Mom shakes her head. "No. We made this decision together."

I'm not sure what to believe.

I can't be here right now, and there's only one place to go. Standing up, I say, "I need some space, too. I'm going to Nora's."

I don't see how my parents react because I rush out the door, letting it slam behind me, the sound echoing down the hallway.

Thankfully, my parents don't follow me out. They're used to me saying I'm going to Nora's. I head downstairs, hoping that nobody else will be in the Hideout, because more than anything, I want to be alone. When I get down there, I breathe a sigh of relief when I see that the lights are off and nobody's there. I never noticed it before, but the inside of the door to the Hideout has a lock. I decide to lock it so none of the other kids will come down here. I can't stand to see anyone right now.

I crawl onto my favorite beanbag chair and grab the fleece blanket that somebody left in a basket on the bottom of the bookshelf. I wrap it around myself and cry. I don't want to go back upstairs yet, so I text my mom.

JOY: going to sleep over at Nora's apt, if that's okay

A few seconds later, my mom responds.

MOM: That's fine. I'm sorry you're so upset. We'll talk some more in the morning.

I turn on my favorite movie score playlist and wrap myself tighter in the blanket. I stare at the messages on the wall that I've been exchanging with the mysterious kid—Oliver?—and wish I could talk to them right now. Writing back and forth to them used to make me feel less alone, but now I know it's all a lie. I still don't know for sure that it's Oliver. But what seems pretty clear is that they don't care about me. I think about them constantly, but they're probably not thinking about me at all.

The truth is, I'm more alone than ever.

Chapter Twenty-One

I *jolt awake when* I hear someone pounding on a door. When I open my eyes I'm disoriented. And then I remember that I'm still in the Hideout. Light streams in through the one open window close to the ceiling. Outside, birds are chirping and cars are whooshing by. It must be morning now. I look at my phone and see that the battery died.

What time is it? I hope it's early enough that my parents aren't looking for me at Nora's. I'd better head back upstairs. I throw the blanket off of me and stand up. My neck hurts a little. Turns out sleeping on a beanbag chair isn't all that comfortable.

Someone is still pounding on the door. Maybe it's Nora or one of the other kids, trying to come down here. They're probably confused about why the door is locked.

"One second." I walk up the stairs and unlock the door. I start pushing it up, but then the person on the other side pulls it. I wait to see a friend's face on the other side of the door.

But once it's all the way open, I see how wrong I am. Because standing there, in the storage closet, looking down at me?

It's my mom.

"Joy!" Mom cries out. "Oh, thank God. We were so worried. What are you doing down here?"

I climb out of the Hideout, and she pulls me into a hug. She squeezes so hard I stop breathing for a second. "I'm so glad you're okay." While still holding onto me, she makes a call on her cell. "Evan? I found her." A pause. "She's fine." Another pause. "Yeah, let Felix know. We'll be right up."

She hangs up the phone and releases me from the hug, but holds onto my arms. "Don't you *ever* do that to us again."

"I'm so sorry," I say. "I didn't mean to scare you.

Wait—is Dad home?" There's a glimmer of hope in my gut as I imagine Dad deciding not to stay at Uncle Spencer's after all.

"He came back when I realized you weren't at Nora's apartment," Mom says.

"Oh." I try to close the door to the Hideout so we can leave, but Mom stops me.

"Wait. What is down there?" she asks.

"Nothing," I say automatically. The lie makes me break into a sweat, but there's no way Mom can see what's down there. It's bad enough that she discovered the secret door. Grown-ups aren't supposed to know about the Hideout at all.

"Joy. Move out of the way. Right now." It's clear from the tone in Mom's voice that she is not going to let this go.

I slowly move to the side of the Hideout door. Mom crouches over and lifts it up again, and then peers inside. "What is down there?" she repeats.

I don't say anything.

"Joy? What. Is. Down. There?"

"A room, okay! It's no big deal."

"Show me."

"You don't have to go down there. I'm sorry. I'll never do anything like this again, I promise. You can forget about it." The words tumble out quickly.

"I'm not going to forget it because you were down there all night when you were supposed to be at Nora's apartment. Show me the room. Now."

I walk down the steps and turn on the light switch. Mom is right behind me.

"What is this place?" Mom asks when she's down the steps, too.

"It's a room where the kids in the building hang out. That's it. Can we go now?"

Mom ignores my question. "Why didn't you tell me about it?"

"It's, um, supposed to be a secret."

Mom glares at me and then peers around the room, as if she's trying to make sense of it all. She sees the fleece blanket on the beanbag chair. "Is that where you slept?"

I nod. "How did you find me?"

"I stopped by Nora's apartment this morning when I didn't hear from you. And Felix let me know that you weren't there, that you hadn't been there all night. I was terrified and called your dad immediately. Do you understand what you put us through?" Mom's voice breaks a little, and my heart sinks.

"I'm sorry, Mom. I just wanted to be by myself for a little while."

Mom continues as if she hadn't heard me. "I turned

on the tracker that tells us where your phone is, and it said the last location was down here. It kept telling me the phone had been in this closet, but I couldn't find it, or you. Then I found that door. I started banging on it because I didn't know what else to do." She sounds like she's about to cry.

I can't even look at Mom in the eyes. "I'm sorry," I say again.

"Let's go upstairs," Moms says. "Your dad is waiting for us. We'll talk more in our apartment."

I close the Hideout door before following Mom upstairs. The dread in my chest grows bigger with every step I take.

Dad hugs me tight as soon as I walk in the door. "I'm so glad you're okay."

"I'm fine," I say. "Sorry I scared you."

When he finally lets go of me, he says, "Have a seat on the couch."

"Where's Malia?" I ask.

"In her room," Dad says. "Playing with her Legos so we can talk."

I nod and take a deep breath. I don't know what's going to happen next, but it's not going to be good. I've never been in this much trouble before.

"I'm so glad you're safe," Dad says. "But what you did was unacceptable. And dangerous. Do you understand?"

I nod. "I know. I promise, I didn't mean to scare you. Either of you."

"But you lied to us. On purpose," Mom says.

"I wanted to be alone, and I knew you wouldn't follow me if I said I was going to Nora's house."

"This is serious, Joy," Mom says. "What if you'd gotten hurt down there? You can't go to some secret room and not tell anyone."

"What secret room?" Dad asks.

Mom explains where she found me, giving him details about what the room looks like.

I cringe while listening to her describe the Hideout, a place that's supposed to be only for the kids in the building. This was the biggest Hideout rule, and I broke it. I can't let the other kids find out, or they'll hate me.

"Does Carlos know about it?" Dad asks.

My eyes get wide. "No! You can't tell Carlos. You can't tell anyone."

"Excuse me, but you are not the parent here," Mom says. "You do not tell us what to do."

This is bad. *Really* bad. If Carlos finds out about the Hideout, he'll probably close off the room for good. I don't want to lose the Hideout. I don't want all the other

167

kids to hate me! I'll lose all of them, I know it.

Tears fill my eyes. "Please. I know I messed up. But you can't tell anyone else about the Hideout. It's supposed to be a secret."

"The Hideout? Who else knows about this room, Joy?" Mom asks.

Shoot. Now they know what we call it. What is *wrong* with me?

"Joy?" Mom repeats. There's a warning in her tone.

"My other friends in the building," I finally say, my voice low.

"The kids you hang out with at the bus stop?" Dad asks me.

I nod.

"We should talk to their parents," Mom says to Dad.

"Please." I look down at my lap and blink a lot so I won't cry. "Please don't."

"You can go to your room now," Mom says. "We need to talk about your punishment."

Telling other people about the Hideout is punishment enough, but of course I don't say that out loud.

I go to my room. Malia is sitting on the rug surrounded by a million Lego pieces. "Look, I made a butterfly rocket. Want to see?"

"Not right now," I mumble. I climb up to the top bunk

and stare at the ceiling while I wait for my parents to be done talking.

They come into the room a few minutes later and stand next to the bunk bed. With me lying down and them standing up, we're face-to-face.

"We're taking your phone away when you're at home. You can only have it at school, so we can reach you. Same with your laptop—you can only use it for homework, with supervision. You also can't get together with your friends for two weeks. The only thing we're letting you do is walk the dogs, since you made a commitment to Nora and the dog owners."

I nod. At least I can still see Nora. Hopefully she will still want to talk to me after she hears what happened.

Then Dad says, "We have no choice but to tell the other parents and Carlos about the room downstairs. We don't even know if that room is safe to inhabit, if it's structurally sound. And if the other kids are going down there, their parents should know."

I want to yell, tell them they can't do this, but I know it's no use. They've made up their minds, and arguing with them will only make my punishment worse.

When Mom and Dad leave, Malia stares up at me with wide eyes, her butterfly rocket frozen in midair. "Whoa, Joy. What did you *do?*"

"Nothing." I turn around so I'm facing the wall.

Maybe I can explain it to the other kids. They'll have to understand that I didn't mean for this to happen.

But then I think of what the Hideout means to each of them—a place to draw freely, a place to get away from annoying siblings, a place to be themselves.

Nausea sets in.

What if I just took all of that away from them?

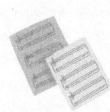

Chapter Twenty-Two

It's official. The Hideout is closed.

Mom and Dad talked to Carlos, and now he's going to tell the other parents in the building about the secret room underneath the storage closet. Carlos is going to add a new lock to the outside of the door while he figures out what to do about it. He'll be the only one with the key.

The Fabulous Five won't be able to escape to the Hideout ever again.

There's nothing that I can do to stop any of this from happening. All I can do is cry. But not for long, because

I have to take Ziggy on his morning walk. He's the only dog Nora and I walk on the weekends. Nora could probably walk him on her own, now that we've had so much practice, but I'm glad my parents are still letting me go. Other than Ziggy's walks, I'm supposed to stay inside the apartment for the rest of the weekend.

But that's okay. What matters is that I have the chance to tell Nora what happened, before she hears it from Carlos or her parents. If I can't talk to all of the other kids right now, at least I can talk to her. I hope she understands that I didn't mean for any of this to happen.

I take a quick shower and change my clothes before heading out.

Nora's getting off the elevator, and I brace myself for her reaction to the Hideout stuff. Maybe she's already heard by now.

But her reaction doesn't come.

"Hey!" she says, sounding normal. "Did you see my text? Did you know your mom thought you were sleeping over at my place last night? What was that about?"

"Yeah . . . about that . . ." I trail off, not sure how to start.

Just then, Mae opens her apartment door. "Good morning, girls," she says. She's smiling, and as usual, Ziggy is beside her wearing his harness, all ready to go.

"Morning," we both say back.

I'm grateful that Mae doesn't know that I'm in trouble. Neither does Ziggy, who comes over and licks my hand. "How's your knee?" I ask.

"Getting better every day," Mae says. "Thank you for asking. Here you go." She passes me and Nora our payment for the week.

I thank her and stuff the twenty-dollar bill in my pocket, like Nora.

"Be back soon," Nora says as we take Ziggy's leash.

The sky is thick with gray clouds.

"Are you going to tell me what's going on now?" Nora asks as we walk. "Why'd your mom think you were at my apartment?"

"Nora, I did something bad."

Her eyes widen. "What?"

"I . . . sort of . . . fell asleep," I say. "In the Hideout. Overnight."

"You *what*?" Nora stops walking, and Ziggy, who was a few steps ahead, gets tugged by his leash as a result.

"I didn't mean to! My parents told me that my dad is moving out."

Nora frowns. "Oh no, I'm sorry."

"Yeah, and I got upset and wanted to be alone. I told my parents that I was going to your apartment, but I really went to the Hideout. I was there for a while, and I didn't want to go home. So I told them I was sleeping at your house. I didn't think they'd come looking for me there. They never did that before."

"Oh."

We get to the park, and Ziggy immediately finds his favorite tree.

While he does his business, I say, "That's not the worst part." I pace next to the tree because I'm too anxious to stand still. "Promise you'll still be my friend after you hear what happened next."

"Uh-oh," Nora says.

"Promise!"

"Okay, I promise. I'm not going to stop being your friend."

I take a deep breath and say, "My mom found me. She found the Hideout."

"What?"

I explain how my phone died, and Mom turned on the "find my phone" app once she realized I wasn't at Nora's apartment. That she tracked me down to the storage closet and found the secret door. I tell her everything that happened after that.

"It's over," I say. "Nora, we can't use the Hideout anymore. Carlos is going to lock it up for good."

She puts her hand over her mouth. My stomach drops and a couple of tears fall from my eyes. But instead of yelling at me, like I was afraid of, Nora comes closer and gives me a hug.

"Do you hate me?" I ask.

"No," she says. "This stinks. But you didn't mean for it to happen. I believe you."

As soon as I hear those words, I feel lighter.

"I'm sorry your dad's moving out," Nora adds.

I nod and get quiet. Then I say, "I'm worried the other kids are going to hate me. I mean, the Hideout was our sanctuary, and now it's gone."

"No," Nora says, but she doesn't sound super convinced. "Don't worry, we'll talk to them."

"I'm not allowed to talk to anyone. I'm only allowed to leave our apartment to walk Ziggy. Until school on Monday."

"Well, maybe it's good if you're not around when they find out."

"Can you explain it to them?" I ask. "Tell them I didn't mean for any of this to happen?"

"I'll try," she says.

I wipe my eyes with the back of my hand and then wipe the dampness off on my shorts. "Why are you being so understanding?"

"Because you're my friend. And my business partner. We're in this together."

"You're the best."

Ziggy, done doing his business, looks up at us expectantly.

"I'll get this one," Nora says, grabbing a baggie.

"No." I take the bag from her. "If anyone deserves to pick up dog poop, it's me."

When we're walking again, Nora says, "Maybe there's a way to get the Hideout back. We can talk to our parents, and to Carlos. Convince them to let us use it again."

"You think that could work?"

"It's worth a try. We could put together another presentation, with our list of reasons."

I nod. Nora's right. Maybe this can be fixed.

I hold on to that little bit of hope for now.

By the end of the weekend, Dad has moved out of the apartment. When Malia cries, I try to comfort her. At least she can still go to ballet class and on a sleepover at her friend's house. Meanwhile, when I'm not walking Ziggy with Nora, I'm stuck in my room thinking about Dad being gone and what that means. Is divorce next? Mom said no, but I'm not sure I believe her.

I'm also thinking about when I'll get to talk to Elena,

Oliver, and Miles. The only thing I can do to distract myself is work on my piano theory workbook, but even it can't stop me from worrying about what will happen now that everything has changed—again. I thought moving out of our house was the worst thing to happen to me, but I was wrong.

Is this how things will be for me from now on? Am I always going to be losing something?

Any glimmer of hope that my other friends will forgive me disappears when I'm heading to the bus stop on Monday morning.

When I'm still halfway down the block, Nora spots me and runs my way.

"Hey," she says.

"Hey. What's going on?"

"I want to warn you." She glances at our friends waiting at the bus stop and then back at me. "They're not happy."

I look past her at Elena, Oliver, and Miles. Elena's arms are crossed, and when she spots me, her eyes shoot daggers. I've never seen her so angry. Oliver and Miles keep their backs toward me. Can they not even look at me?

My chest gets tight, and I focus on Nora again. "But you talked to them, right?"

"Yeah. I tried to explain that it was all an accident. But

you know how much everyone loved the Hideout. And, like, the one rule was to not let adults find out about it . . ." Nora trails off.

She doesn't have to say anything else. It's exactly what I was afraid of. They hate me.

"They'll get over it eventually," Nora quickly adds. "They'll have to. And, you know, we might be able to convince Carlos to open the room up again. But in the meantime, maybe you should . . . I don't know . . . avoid them."

"What am I supposed to do?" I ask. "I need to get on the bus to school, too."

"I know, but maybe stand over here, and when you see the bus pulling up, then go over," Nora suggests. "I'll stand here with you."

I sit down on the curb, suddenly dizzy. *They don't even want me to stand near them at the bus stop?*

The last few days have already been the worst I've ever experienced.

Now on top of losing everything else, I've lost three of my friends, too.

Chapter Twenty-Three

I hate everything about our new routine. In the morning, Dad comes over to drive Malia to school. Mom is usually on her way out the door to head to the train station, and they only say a quick hello to each other. Malia is always super happy to see Dad, but when he give me a hug, all I can think about is how to make him stay.

When it's time for me to leave for school, I sit on the curb half a block away from the bus stop and the other kids. Everyone stays away from me like I have some contagious disease. Except for Nora. She sits on the curb with me a few of the days, and the other days she stands with everyone else. She says it's because she doesn't want to pick a side. She wants to stay friends with all of us. Our group of five went back to being a group of four so easily, and it's like I was never part of it at all. As I stand away from the other kids, who laugh with each other like normal, I'm full of shame from how I let them down. I wish I could disappear.

When the bus arrives, I get on while avoiding looking at anyone but Nora.

In the afternoons, Dad comes over after picking up Malia, so I see him when I get home from school. I walk the dogs with Nora but come straight home after. At least Dad can still help me and Malia with homework, and make us hot chocolate with extra marshmallows.

But then Mom gets home and Dad leaves. Mom, Malia, and I have dinner, just the three of us. I barely have an appetite, partly because Mom's cooking isn't as good as Dad's. Also because I'm too angry to eat. Mom asks questions about our day, and I give one-word answers, letting Malia do all the talking.

I have nothing better to do after dinner, so I finish my homework, complete a couple of pages in my music theory workbook, and go to bed at the same time as Malia.

Is this what depression feels like? I think about the person I wrote messages to in the Hideout, and wish I could talk to them now. Now I'll never know if it was Oliver or someone else.

When I meet up with Nora to walk Ziggy on Sunday, she tries to reassure me. "I told the others that they should forgive you. I think they will, eventually."

"How do you know?" I ask.

"I can tell."

I shrug. She's probably only saying that to make me feel better.

Nora sighs loudly. "At least you don't have to worry about the person writing you messages on the wall anymore."

"What do you mean?" I ask.

"You know, because the last message said not to worry about her anymore," Nora says. "So she's probably fine now."

"Why are you saying 'she'?" I ask. "I already told you I don't think it's Elena."

"Or him. He. Them," Nora says quickly. "Whoever."

We keep walking, but I narrow my eyes at Nora. "How do you know what the last message said?"

"Because you told me, silly."

I definitely did not tell her. I specifically remember not telling her because I didn't want her to say, once again, that finding out who this person was wasn't important.

"No, I didn't," I say.

Nora is silent, and her face twists like she's thinking. Then she says, "Oh wait, you're right. I read it myself. I remember now. You hadn't brought up the Hideout messages in a while, so when I was down there, I went to the corner and looked myself."

"When? Why didn't you tell me before?"

"I was going to, but I read it, like, the night before you slept down there." She gives a nervous laugh. "I forgot."

The realization slowly spreads throughout my body, giving me goose bumps.

I touch Nora's arm, and she stops walking. "It's you."

"What?"

"You wrote the messages," I say. "The poem."

Nora laughs nervously again. "I did not."

"Yes." My mind races as I think about everything that's happened since I read the poem that first time. "It makes sense. Why you kept dismissing the messages. Why you didn't want to help me figure out who wrote them. It's because it was you all along."

"That's ridiculous," Nora says, but her voice sounds all weird now. And she's not looking me in the eyes. She's staring down at Ziggy, who's using this break in our walk to scratch himself with his back leg.

"Tell me the truth, Nora." I cross my arms.

There's another long stretch of silence. Finally, Nora looks at me.

She exhales. "Fine. It was me."

My mouth drops. I know I just figured it out, but it's still a shock to hear her say it.

"But I didn't mean—" Nora begins, but I cut her off.

"I can't believe you lied to me this whole time!" I say.

"It's not like that!"

"You knew that I was dying to know who this person was," I say. "You let me think it was someone else, when all this time you knew it was you!"

"I'm sorry, okay?" Nora says. "I didn't do it to hurt you."

"Why, then? Why didn't you tell me the truth?"

"I didn't want you, or anyone, to know I wrote that poem. I wasn't even going to write back when you first responded to it, but then I did because you were being nice. And it did help."

"But if you were going through something, why wouldn't you tell me?" I ask. "I've told you all about the stuff with my parents."

"I know."

"Do you not trust me?" I ask.

"Of course I do. I'm still your friend after what

183

happened in the Hideout, right?"

"Then why didn't you tell me?" I can't wrap my head around this. Why lie to me all this time?

"I'm sorry."

"I just . . . I feel like . . ." I don't even know what to say. Everything swirls around my mind like a tornado. My parents separating, the Hideout closing, the other kids hating me. And now Nora's betrayal. "I'm so angry at you."

"That's not fair," Nora says. "I don't have to tell you all of my secrets, okay? Just because we're friends doesn't mean I have to tell you everything."

My mouth drops open again, and we stare at each other, both of us now fuming.

I can't take it anymore, so I yank Ziggy's leash from her. "You can go. I'll finish Ziggy's walk by myself."

Nora doesn't respond. She turns around and walks away.

Chapter Twenty-Four

I beg Dad to drive me to school the next morning so I don't have to face Nora on the bus. It was bad enough having the other kids ignore me. But after my fight with Nora, the thought of standing alone at the bus stop is unbearable.

Dad agrees to drop me off, but he says I still have to take the bus home.

At school, I don't see Nora anywhere in between classes. Not that I mind. At lunch, I avoid the cafeteria and go to the library instead.

Nora's not on the bus after school, but I figure I'll see her when it's time to walk the dogs. It'll be weird to go through our regular dog-walking routine after our fight, but I know this job is too important to both of us, so we'll have to make it work. We can walk the dogs in silence.

I pick up Ziggy from Mae's apartment and head down to the lobby to meet Nora like usual. But she's not down there. She must be running late, so I wait for five minutes.

If I had my phone, I'd text her so I wouldn't have to drag Ziggy all the way back upstairs to knock on her door. I decide to do the next best thing. I bring Ziggy to the vestibule that leads to outside. I look at the wall of buzzers—one for each apartment in the building—and ring the one for 5B. It makes a brrring sound on my end, and I know it sounds kind of like a phone ringing in the apartment. I wait to hear Nora's dad's voice come out of the little speaker, asking who it is. But nobody answers.

I ring the buzzer again, and then again after another minute.

Still nothing.

"Sorry, Ziggy," I tell him as I lead him back inside. "We have to go back upstairs before I can take you out."

When I ring Nora's doorbell, nobody answers. Nobody's home. Ziggy whines a little.

Where is Nora? She wouldn't ditch walking dogs

because of our fight yesterday, would she? That would be so . . . petty. How am I supposed to walk the four dogs without her?

Maybe Dad can help me walk the other two dogs. But then what about Malia? I guess she could come, too, but she'd probably slow us down. Or Dad might tell me that I should skip walking the other three dogs for today.

I don't want to cancel on two of our clients so last minute. What if they think Nora and I are unreliable and decide not to use our services anymore? We only got started. I don't want to lose this job now. Saving for my piano and lessons is all I have right now. It's the only thing I have to look forward to.

Guess I'll have to walk all the dogs by myself.

I take Ziggy down to Carlos's apartment and knock on the door.

"No Nora today?" Carlos asks, when he sees that I'm alone.

"Yeah, just me."

Tank is right there to greet me when we get to his apartment.

"Hey, buddy." Once I get Tank's leash on, I put my left hand through both leash handles and grip the nylon tight. Carlos locks the door, and I lead the two dogs to the elevator, using only one hand to hold the leashes, and so far, it's not so bad.

Once we pick up Rollie and Lillie, I wrap their leashes around my other hand tightly, and I lead all four dogs back downstairs.

"Are you okay walking so many dogs by yourself?" Carlos asks.

I'd be more okay if Nora hadn't ditched me, I think. But I tell Carlos, "Yup."

"Okay. I'll see you when you get back."

I lead the dogs outside. Actually, they end up leading me, since once they get to the lobby and can see outside through the glass door, they pull the leashes toward it. But I manage to keep a good handle on them.

We walk down the block toward the park, stopping constantly so one of the four dogs can pee or poop. I can't figure out how to pick up after them while holding all four leashes, so I make a mental note of where they did their business so I can come back once I'm done walking them. I hope that nobody notices that I'm leaving the poop behind.

That's one of Joyful Dog Walkers' mottos—Leave No Poop Behind. As gross as it sounds, it's something Nora and I pride ourselves on. Who would've thought I'd ever need to say those words? But it's true. Nothing's worse than walking on the sidewalk, or in a park, and realizing there's dog poop on the ground and you've just stepped in it.

I've got to stop thinking about poop. I smile to myself for a second. At least it's taking my mind off of other things.

A few minutes later, the dogs and I are at the entrance to the park. It's gotten really cloudy all of a sudden. If it's going to rain soon, we should take a shorter loop around the park. Hopefully the rain holds out until we're back in our building.

For a while, the walk is going better than I thought. Maybe I can handle more than two dogs on my own, and this summer, Nora and I can sign on even more clients. If she still wants to work with me at all.

But then, once we're halfway around the park's path, I feel a drop of water on my head. Then another on my shoulder. And then several more raindrops.

"Okay, doggies," I say. "Let's walk a little faster."

At first, they don't seem too concerned about the rain, but then it starts to pick up more. Rollie and Lillie pull on their leashes, which almost makes me lose my balance.

"Ack. Okay, we're going," I say to them. I pick up my pace, and Ziggy and Tank keep up behind us.

By the time we get to the park's entrance, it's pouring.

Sheets of rain come down, making the ground slippery. It's hard to see far in front of me. Thankfully I know this route well enough, so we forge ahead.

But then there's a large rumbling sound in the not-too-far distance. Thunder. It's followed by a crash of lightning and more thunder.

The dogs yelp in fear, and the leashes pull away from me. I try to get a better handle on them, but as I'm doing that, thunder booms again. One dog yanks so hard that I let go of one of the leashes. The next thing I know, one of the dogs is running away from us, back into the park, with the leash trailing behind. Through the rain I can immediately tell which dog it is. *Ziggy.*

"Ziggy, no!" I yell. "Come back!" I start pulling the other dogs back toward the park. There's another crash of thunder, and Rollie and Lillie pull me in the direction of our building. Together, the two of them are strong. There's no way I can pull them back into the park in this rain to find Ziggy.

No, no, no, no. What do I do? I have to go get Ziggy! I can't leave him.

But I'm not going to be able to run back to the park with these other dogs. I debate tying their leashes to a bench, but I'm not sure I'll be able to tie them tight enough, especially with wet hands. No, what I should do is get these three dogs back to the building, and then come back out to find Ziggy by myself. He can't have gone far, not in this rain. He probably ran to find shelter. Maybe he's under another park bench, or in the covered picnic area. He's probably waiting for someone to come rescue him.

Stay put, Ziggy, I think as I hurry back toward the building with the other dogs. *I'll be right back to get you.*

I don't let myself think the worst: What if Ziggy's gone?

Chapter Twenty-Five

I hold the other three leashes as tight as I can as the dogs and I run back to the apartment building. With every step I take, my sneakers squeak from all the water in my socks. When we get to the covered front entrance of the building, Tank, Rollie, and Lillie all shake themselves to dry off, getting me wetter in the process. I wring out my T-shirt and wipe my face with the back of my hand. My hair is sopping wet, too, so I quickly squeeze out as much water as I can.

We go inside and head straight to Carlos's door. I hope we can return the dogs to their apartments quickly so I can go back to the park.

"I was wondering if you got caught in the rain," Carlos says, when he sees how wet I am. "Everything okay? Do you need something to dry off?"

"No, I'm okay," I lie. "It's just a little water."

Carlos stares at the dogs beside me. "Where's Ziggy?"

"Oh. I dropped him off already," I lie again. I don't want to admit that I lost Ziggy. If I can find him right away, then nobody has to know.

"All right, well, let's get these other dogs home," Carlos says. "Want to borrow a towel to dry them off?"

I don't want to take the time to dry the dogs off, not when Ziggy is still out there, but I also don't think it'll be good for business to leave wet dogs at my clients' apartments. "That'd be great," I say. I'll have to be quick.

Carlos gets a couple of towels, and we do our best to dry off the dogs before dropping them off to their apartments.

"Have a good night," Carlos says. He heads to the stairwell to go back downstairs.

I wait a few seconds and then stand at the top of the stairwell until I hear that Carlos is back on the first floor. When I'm pretty sure he must be back in his apartment, I run down to the lobby and outside.

By now the rain has started to let up. Thank goodness, because I still don't have an umbrella or rain jacket. I can't waste any more time before finding Ziggy. I hope I'm not too late.

I run all the way back to the park. "Ziggy!" I yell as I jog around it. I crouch down to check under every bench and picnic table, and circle each tree.

When I get to the building with the public bathrooms, I go inside the ladies' room and check all of the stalls. I don't want to go into the men's room, so I crack the door and call Ziggy's name. I don't hear anything, and Ziggy probably couldn't have opened the door to get inside anyway.

I stand on a picnic table and scan the park, hoping to see Ziggy huddled somewhere. But he's nowhere to be found.

What else can I do? Think, Joy.

The security guard! I run to the booth next to the parking lot.

"Excuse me, sir?" I ask the man sitting inside. "Have you seen a tan French bulldog?"

He's holding a walkie-talkie, which beeps and makes a static sound. "A French bulldog? Can't say I have." Then someone starts talking on the walkie, and the security guard lifts it closer to his ear.

I leave the park.

Where could Ziggy have gone?

What if he's hurt?

What if someone took him?

What am I going to do?

How am I going to tell Mae that I lost her dog? Her sweet Ziggy?

Tears re-wet my face as I walk back to the building. I call for Ziggy along the way. Maybe he decided to leave the park when the rain stopped, so he could get back home.

I walk around the building, checking all around the parking lot and under each car. But I can't find him anywhere.

I have no choice. I can't find Ziggy on my own. I have to go tell Mae.

I take the stairs to Mae's door. I'm shaking as I ring her doorbell, and as I wait for Mae to come.

"I'm glad you made it back inside," Mae says as she's opening the door. "That storm came out of nowhere." Then she sees the expression on my face. "What on earth is wrong?" Her eyes move to the floor, where she's expecting to see Ziggy. But he's not there.

My vision blurs with tears as I make myself say the words out loud. "I . . . I lost him. Ziggy. When the rain and thunder started, he got scared and I lost control of his . . . leash . . . and he ran off. I couldn't get to him fast enough. I had the other dogs with me, so I had to come back here to drop them off. But I went back out to look for Ziggy . . . and . . ." I hiccup. "He's nowhere."

Mae puts her hand on her chest, and for a minute, I'm terrified that I'm giving her an actual heart attack.

"Oh my god," Mae says. "Oh no. Ziggy."

She looks at me. "Listen, I know this isn't your fault. This was too big a responsibility for a child."

I don't know how to respond. I'm almost a teenager. But then again, I did lose Ziggy.

Nora was supposed to be there with me. If she were, this never would've happened.

"Why don't you go change into dry clothes?" Mae says. "Are your parents around?"

I nod. "My dad. I came straight here, so he doesn't know what happened yet."

"Okay. I'm going to call my son and see if he can go out and look for Ziggy. Go tell your dad and change out of your wet clothes. Then come back and tell me everything that happened."

I nod, grateful that Mae has taken control of the situation.

I close Mae's apartment door and stand in front of mine. My hands shake as I put my key into the lock. When I get inside, it's quiet, and now that the rain is gone, birds are chirping again outside. Why did the weather have to betray me like this?

Malia runs in from our room, holding her homework folder. "You're all wet."

Dad pokes his head out of the kitchen. When he sees me, his face shifts to concern. "You okay, Joy?"

"Dad." I gulp. "Something bad happened."

Chapter Twenty-Six

I immediately run over to Dad and bury my face in his chest. I'm so glad he's here right now. My tears start up again as I tell him everything that happened.

"I can't believe I lost Ziggy," I say.

He rubs my back. "It was an accident."

"It's okay, Joy," Malia says, hugging me from behind. "I bet Ziggy knows how to get home."

"Mae is really upset," I say. "I should never have taken all of the dogs out without Nora."

"What do you mean?" Dad asks, leaning back so he can see my face. "Where was Nora?"

"I don't know. She wasn't home, so I had to walk the dogs myself."

Dad frowns. "You know we didn't want you walking dogs by yourself. You should've told me. I could've helped."

He's right. I should've asked for his help, even if that meant Malia tagging along. "Am I in trouble?"

"No. You didn't mean to lose Ziggy. We're going to figure this out. He'll turn up. He couldn't have gone far."

I nod.

"Go dry off, and then we'll go talk to Mae," Dad says.

I go into the bathroom to change. My hair is a total mess, so I wrap one of Mom's scarves around it. Then the three of us go back over to Mae's apartment.

"Hi, Mae. I'm so sorry about what happened," Dad says, when she opens the door.

"It's all right. We'll figure this out. Come on in, and I'll call John back."

We sit on her couch while Mae calls her son back and puts the phone on speaker. I hear John clear his throat on the other end.

"Okay, Joy," Mae says. "Please tell us exactly what happened."

I take a deep breath and tell her the whole story. I stare

at my lap while I talk, too ashamed to look at Mae and see her expression. But when I'm done explaining what happened, I sneak a glance at her. She has a very worried look on her face.

"Okay, the first thing I'm going to do is give all of the local animal shelters a call," John says from the other end of the line. "That way if he turns up at any of those places, they'll know to call us."

My chest tightens. I imagine Ziggy still feeling cold and wet from the rain, since he doesn't have a towel to dry off with. He's probably hungry, too, since it's getting to be dinnertime.

The guilt overwhelms me.

I know Mae said what happened isn't my fault, but she was probably saying that to be nice. This is all my fault.

"Thank you, John," Mae says.

"I don't know what you were thinking, letting a kid walk Ziggy," John says. "Purebred French bulldogs aren't cheap."

My face burns. I look over at Dad, whose expression hardens.

"It's not about the money," Mae says. "It's about getting Ziggy home safe. And I adopted him, John. You know that."

Mae looks at me like she's finally realizing my family

doesn't need to hear this part of the conversation. "I'll call you back," she says before hanging up the phone.

"I'm so sorry," I say.

Dad stands up, which makes me and Malia stand up, too. "Please let us know if there's anything we can do."

"I will."

"I can go back outside and look for Ziggy again if you want," I say.

"No, you've done enough," Mae says. It's a punch to my gut. "John is going to come over and look. You can go on home."

"Okay."

As we're walking out, I hear Mae calling John back.

"It's me again," she says, and then after a pause, she says. "Yes, I know that."

When we're back at our apartment, I don't know what to do with myself. I should do my homework, or study for the science final, but there's no way I can focus on any of that right now. Instead, I go out onto the small terrace and sit on the folding chair we have out there. I peer down at the front of our building, hoping that I'll see Ziggy trotting back home.

He's a smart dog. He has to know his way back home. He's been to the park so many times.

But what if he got hurt? What if while he was running

away after hearing the thunder, he fell down and hurt himself? Or what if someone took him and isn't planning to bring him back?

After a while, Dad opens the terrace door. "How about some hot chocolate?"

"Okay."

"I want some, too!" Malia yells from behind him.

"Two hot chocolates, coming up," Dad says.

I come back inside and sit on the couch while Dad goes into the kitchen. Malia sits next to me and starts telling me about something funny that happened at school. I pretend to listen.

A couple of minutes later, Dad comes back out with two mugs of hot chocolate with lots of mini marshmallows on top, plus two spoons. It's just like he always makes it.

"Yum!" Malia uses the spoon to scoop a couple of mini marshmallows off the top and eats them.

"Give it a second to cool off," Dad says.

I take a sip anyway, and it burns my tongue. I totally deserve it.

Mom comes home from work an hour later. When she sees the expression on my face as I'm sitting on the couch next to Dad, she frowns.

"What's wrong?" she asks.

For the third time, I tell the story of what happened this afternoon.

"Oh, Joy," Mom says, shaking her head. "Oh, honey." She comes over and gives me a hug.

Then she looks at Dad.

"Joy, why don't you go to your room so your dad and I can talk for a minute."

"Okay." I go to my room and close the door. I expect to hear my parents start fighting, but that's not what happens. Well, if they are fighting, they're doing it with low voices.

This is what I've wanted—for them to both be here, and not fighting. But losing Ziggy wasn't supposed to be part of it.

I take my homework out of my backpack and try to focus on it. I'm in the middle of a math problem when my parents appear at my doorway.

"Hey, Joy," Mom says. "We want to talk to you about something."

"Okay."

They come inside, and I swivel around in my desk chair so I'm facing them.

"We think that you should put your dog-walking business on hold for now," Mom says.

"What?" I look at Dad. "You said I wasn't in trouble."

"You're not," Dad says. "We thought you could handle

walking these dogs, but it seems like it's too much."

"I can handle it. It's not too much when Nora and I are doing it together."

"I know, but Nora wasn't there today," Dad says. "What if she misses other days? It's too much of a responsibility for you."

"We don't want . . . ," Mom begins and then pauses. "We want you to take a break. Until you're older."

I know what she wants to say. They don't want me to lose any more dogs.

Then I realize something. Mae's son John said French bulldogs are expensive. If Ziggy isn't found, what if Mae sues us? Would we have to get a lawyer? Would my parents have to pay Mae any money? They wouldn't be able to afford any of that.

The weight of what I've done feels even heavier.

Mom and Dad are right. I can't walk any more dogs, it's too much of a risk. And I *have* to find Ziggy.

If Ziggy isn't found, I can already think of three terrible consequences. I make a list in my head.

1. I'll have to live with this guilt forever.
2. I won't be able to work to save up for a piano or lessons.

And more important, 3. I will have made everything a million times worse for my family.

Chapter Twenty-Seven

When I wake up the next morning, the first thought that goes through my mind is that I hope Ziggy is back with Mae. I hope that somehow he made it back home overnight.

Mom is in the kitchen, all dressed for work and pouring coffee into her travel mug. It's weird not having Dad here making coffee with her, and helping make Malia's and my school lunches. Mom started making our lunches at night, and leaving them in the fridge for us to grab before school.

"Morning, sweetie," she says.

"Morning. Have you heard anything about Ziggy?"

"Not yet." She comes over and gives me a kiss on the forehead. "But I'm sure we'll hear something soon. I'm off to the train. Your dad will be here in a few minutes to take Malia to school, okay?"

"Okay," I say. It seems like Mom is always rushing off to work lately.

"Have a good day."

Today, I'm actually looking forward to getting on the bus. I need to talk to Nora as soon as possible. I need to know why she abandoned me yesterday. And if she doesn't already know about Ziggy, I need to tell her what happened.

Dad shows up when I'm getting dressed for school. I eat a bowl of cereal with him and Malia, and then head out. When I get into the hallway, part of me wants to knock on Mae's door to find out if Ziggy is there. But if he still hasn't been found, I don't want to face Mae again so soon.

I take a few steps toward the elevator but then stop. What if Ziggy is back home? I look around to make sure the coast is clear, and then put my ear against Mae's door. I don't expect to hear any barking, since Ziggy's pretty quiet, but maybe I'll hear the jingling of his collar, or the squeak of a toy in his mouth. Or the pitter-patter of him walking across the room. Something doglike.

But I can't hear anything. I'll have to get an update some other way. Maybe Carlos knows something.

I head to the elevator and press the down button. When the door opens, there's Nora, leaning against the back wall of the elevator, with her Mets hat on, looking down at something on her phone. It's like the first time I talked to her, the day my family first moved in. That feels like forever ago now.

Nora glances up for a second, but when she sees it's me, she goes back to looking at her phone.

I rush inside. "Oh my gosh, Nora. Where were you yesterday?"

She doesn't say anything. The elevator door closes, and we start moving.

"You left me hanging with the dogs," I say. "Why didn't you tell me you couldn't make it?"

She finally looks up at me. "I'm sorry."

"Do you know what happened?" I ask.

"With Zig? Yeah, I heard."

"How'd you find out?"

"Your dad came over last night and told my dad," she says.

"Oh. He didn't tell me that." Dad must've stopped by as he was leaving for Uncle Spencer's.

"He told my dad that he doesn't want you to do the

dog-walking business anymore," Nora adds. "So Dad doesn't want me to do it either. And I'm in trouble for ditching you."

I nod, not surprised. But it still stinks. My sadness from yesterday morphs into anger. Anger at Nora for not being there yesterday. All of this could've been avoided.

The elevator arrives in the lobby, and we both get off. I follow Nora toward the front door of the building.

"Why did you ditch me?" I ask.

She stops walking and looks at me. "You told me to leave when we were walking Zig. You didn't need me anymore."

"That one time!" I say. "Of course I needed you to walk all four dogs."

"I know that, all right?" She exhales loudly. "I already feel bad that Zig's lost somewhere, and I got a huge lecture from my dad. You don't have to make me feel worse."

"I'm just telling the truth. This was your business, too, and we were supposed to work together." I pause. "And, you know, we wouldn't have gotten in a fight in the first place if you were honest with me about the Hideout messages."

Nora squeezes her eyes shut and then opens them again. "You're never going to get over that, are you?"

"I thought we were better friends than that," I say. "I

told you what was going on with me, and I thought you'd talk to me about your stuff, too."

"You want to know what the poem was about? Why I wrote it?" Nora asks. "It's because I got my period. My first one ever. And it was *horrible*." Then she bursts into tears.

My mouth drops open.

Nora keeps talking. "My dad was a disaster. He didn't know what to do, how to help me. It made me miss my mom." Her voice breaks a little, and she clears her throat. "I didn't say anything because the whole thing was so embarrassing. But you want to know what's going on with me? I miss my dead mom, okay? I wish she was here, but she's not, and she's never going to come back. So there you have it. You know my secret now. Are you happy?"

I shake my head. "Of course not. I'm so sorry."

Nora wipes her face with her sleeve. "Now you know."

Before I can say anything else, she turns around and pushes the door to outside, hard, so it swings open. And then she's gone.

Chapter Twenty-Eight

I can't stop thinking about my argument with Nora. Now that I know what happened, why she wrote that poem in the first place, I feel awful. All this time, I wanted to know who was writing the messages so I could help them. So we could help each other. But all I've done is make things worse for her.

I think about what she went through, how hard it must be to not have her mom around when she needs her the most. It stinks that my dad isn't living with us, but at least he's only a short drive away. I haven't gotten my period yet, but I can't imagine not being able to go to my mom for help.

How can I make things right with Nora?

I want to figure all of this out, but first I need to find Ziggy. He's still out there, and he could be hurt—or worse. But I can't think that way. He has to be okay, wherever he is. I have to do whatever it takes to find him. Then once he's home, I will find a way to show Nora how sorry I am. Maybe finding Ziggy will help fix things between us, because she cares about him, too. Then we can convince our parents to let us walk dogs again, and she can keep saving up for her camera and shoot her movie.

While I'm doing homework on my computer after school, I look up how to find lost dogs. Immediately, an article pops up with a list of steps. The first one is what Mae's son, John, said he was going to do—contact the local shelters. I wonder if anything came up when he called. I guess not, or Ziggy would be home right now.

The next step is to search the neighborhood. The article says to do it several times a day. I wonder if Mae or John have been able to do this. Probably not Mae, since her knee is still bothering her.

Well, I have more time on my hands now, so I can do it. Starting right now.

I go into the living room, where Dad is helping Malia with her homework.

"Is it okay if I walk to the park?" I ask him. "I want

to look around for Ziggy again. Maybe there's some clue about where he could've gone. I'll come home right after."

"We'll come with you," Dad says. "Three pairs of eyes are better than one."

The three of us head outside. It's a beautiful day—sunny and pleasant. But I can't enjoy it, not when Ziggy's still lost.

"Can I go on the swings?" Malia asks, when we get to the park and she spots the playground.

"Let's look for Ziggy first," Dad says.

We walk around both the small and big loops, searching every nook and cranny. But there's no sign of Ziggy anywhere.

"Sorry we didn't find him," Dad says as we're walking back to the building, after Malia and I went on the swings.

"I'll search again tomorrow," I say.

When I'm back in my room, I return to the article from before.

It says the third step to finding a lost dog is to advertise. Put notices around the neighborhood, as well as in grocery stores, community centers, veterinary offices, and pet supply stores.

I can totally create a flyer. I even have the perfect picture of Ziggy, which I took during one of our walks. I open a new document on my computer, insert the picture in the middle of the page, and type LOST DOG in big red letters on the top. On the bottom, I put more details about Ziggy—his sex, age, breed, and color. I don't know his weight, so I leave that off.

I don't have a color printer at home, but I print a copy in black and white. Then I decide to go next door to check with Mae, to see if she's okay with me hanging them up.

I hesitate before ringing Mae's doorbell. She has to still be mad at me. But finding Ziggy is more important than my feelings, so I take a deep breath and knock.

A minute later, Mae opens it, still holding her cane.

"Hi, Joy." She doesn't look angry, but she's also not her usual chipper self.

"Hi. Um, I wanted to show you this." I hold up the flyer. "I didn't know if you or your son had already made flyers."

"Actually, no," Mae says. "Not yet. Can I see it?"

I hand it over. "If it's okay with you, I'll put your phone number on the flyer and print a bunch of copies in color. I can ask my dad to help me hang them up everywhere."

"That's kind of you," Mae says.

"It's the least I can do."

Mae nods. "You can add my phone number. Thank you for doing this."

"You're welcome." I give a small smile, grateful that I'm able to help. I hope this works.

Uncle Spencer has a color printer, so when Dad comes by the next day, he brings over some copies. He also offers to hang them up around town. In the meantime, I tape the flyers next to each elevator and stairwell on every floor in our building.

When I get to the fifth floor, I wonder if I'll see Nora coming out of her apartment. I haven't bumped into her in the building since our fight, and she's been avoiding me everywhere else. She sits next to Oliver on the bus, so I sit alone. When I first tried to talk to her, she turned her back to me and started a conversation with Oliver. In the cafeteria at school, Nora and the other broadcasting club kids gave me dirty looks when I walked up to their table. I didn't know what else to do, so I started eating lunch in the library, alone.

I know I messed up, but do I really deserve all of this?

When I'm done hanging up the flyers, I stand in front of Nora's door, debating whether I should knock. After a minute, I take a deep breath and do it.

I'm surprised when Nora opens the door. I was expecting her dad. She immediately frowns at me. "What do you want?"

"I'm so glad you answered," I say. "I'm really, really

sorry, Nora. About everything."

"Okay." She doesn't look convinced.

"Do you believe me?" I ask. "I feel so terrible."

Nora looks down at her feet. "I don't want to talk to you right now."

"Wait," I say, before she can close the door on me.

She looks at me, but I don't know what else to say, how to make it up to her. I take one of the flyers and hand it to her. "I made these. To find Ziggy."

She takes the flyer and, without another word, closes the door.

For a minute, I stand there, staring at it.

There has to be some way to show Nora how sorry I am, how much our friendship means to me. I need to figure out how to make this right again.

I hope by the time I do, it's not too late.

Chapter Twenty-Nine

"I need your help with something," I tell Mom the following night. She's in her room sorting laundry into piles.

She pauses to talk to me. "Sure, what do you need?"

"I want to do more to help find Ziggy," I say.

"Understandable," Mom says. "We all want Ziggy to be found."

"I was thinking, what if I organize a bigger search party? I could get other people in the building to sign up. We could break up into groups, spread out around the neighborhood, and knock on people's doors. Ziggy has to be out there somewhere. If the local shelters haven't seen him, then maybe someone else found him. Or maybe someone else—outside the park—has seen him somewhere. It's worth a try. Please, will you let me?"

"That's a great idea," Mom says. "Of course I'll help."

I hug her. "Thank you. If I make some new flyers with the search party info, will you come with me to hand them out around the building?"

"Absolutely."

"Also, I was thinking maybe we can draw people in with the promise of food. Like order some pizzas for the volunteers. Everyone loves free food. I can use some of my dog-walking money to pay for it. It's worth it." At this point, I'll do anything to get Ziggy back.

"I don't want you to use your own money," Mom says. "I can pitch in for that."

"Are you sure we can . . . you know . . . afford it?" I ask.

"We can afford a few pizzas," Mom says.

"Thank you! I'll go design the flyer."

Mom starts sorting laundry again, and I go back into my room. I open up a new document on my computer, put Ziggy's picture in the middle again, but instead of writing LOST DOG on the top, I type HELP US FIND ZIGGY in large letters. Then below the picture, I write, "Join us on Saturday, June 20, at 3:00 p.m. to search for fellow friend and neighbor Ziggy (apartment 3D). All volunteers will get pizza after the search!"

Once I'm happy with it, I show it to Mae to make sure she's okay with it. She is, so I print a bunch of copies from our home printer. I figure black-and-white copies will work fine.

Mom and I decide to go around the building and hand out the flyers the following night, around eight o'clock. We figure most people will be done with dinner by then. Malia comes with us, but she insists on wearing her pajamas since it's right before her bedtime. They're pink and covered with smiling rainbows.

"I want to press the buttons," Malia says as we head to the elevator. "All of them."

"Deal," I say.

We start with 1A, and Malia rings the doorbell. The last time I saw Carlos was when I lied about dropping off Ziggy the night I lost him. What if Carlos calls me out on it?

When he opens the door a few moments later, I brace myself.

But all he says is, "Oh hi." He seems surprised to see us. "Everything okay? Do you need help with something in your apartment?"

"No, it's nothing like that," Mom says.

"We wanted to give you this." I hand over a flyer. "We're putting together a search party to look for Ziggy." I pause, and then blurt out, "I'm sorry about lying to you. I hadn't dropped off Ziggy that night. He was already lost, but I panicked when you asked me about him."

"It's okay," Carlos says, his expression sympathetic. "I understand."

Relieved, I explain my search party plan and tell him that there will be pizza afterward.

"That's a great idea," Carlos says. "If you need help handing out the rest of the flyers, I can slip them in everyone's mailboxes."

"That would save us a lot of time." Mom puts her arm around Malia. "This one needs to go to bed soon."

"Of course."

I hand over the pile of flyers. "Thank you so much! Can we count you in for the search?"

"My family will be there," Carlos says.

I grin. "Awesome."

Hopefully the rest of our neighbors will agree to come help, too.

"That worked out nicely," Mom says as we're getting in the elevator to head back upstairs. Malia presses the button for our floor.

"Thanks for coming with me to hand out the flyers," I say.

"You're welcome, honey."

"Is it okay if I invite Dad to the search party, too?"

"Of course!"

I smile. "Great. I know Carlos is going to make sure everyone gets a flyer, but can I still give a few out myself? I can do it quickly while you get Malia ready for bed."

"Nora?" Mom asks.

I shake my head. "She doesn't want to talk to me. We got into a fight, and I hurt her feelings. I didn't mean for it to happen."

"Sorry to hear that," Mom says.

"I don't know if she'll ever forgive me."

"I'm sure she will," Mom says. "You two were such good friends. Just give her some time."

"Yeah."

"So who do you want to give flyers to?" Mom asks.

"The other kids—Miles, Elena, and Oliver." They're still avoiding me at the bus stop, but maybe if I talk to them alone, they'll be willing to forgive me.

"Fine," Mom says. "But bring your phone with you, and be home in twenty minutes. That should be more than enough time."

"Deal."

Unlike Nora, I'm terrible at memorizing people's apartment numbers, so I look at the directory in the lobby's vestibule. Oliver is 2F, Elena is 4E, and Miles is 5D. I decide to start at the lowest floor and work my way up.

Oliver's door has a pretty spring wreath on it, with branches forming a circle and small white flowers and leaves on the bottom half. I take a deep breath and ring the doorbell.

A minute later, Oliver opens the door.

"Joy," he says. "What are you doing here?"

"Hey." I hold up my flyer. "I wanted to give you this. I'm putting together a search party to find Ziggy. I don't know if you heard—"

Oliver cuts me off. "Yeah, Nora told us."

I wonder what she told them about our fight. "I hope you'll come," I say. "If not for me, then for Nora. She cares about Ziggy, too."

"I'll be there," he says without hesitation.

"Great." Hope flutters in my belly. Maybe Oliver can forgive me. "Listen, I'm so sorry about what happened in the Hideout. I promise I didn't mean for any of that to happen."

Oliver shrugs. "It's okay. I'm not really mad at you."

"You're not?"

"I'm disappointed we can't use the Hideout anymore. But it was probably only a matter of time before we were caught down there."

"Then why aren't you talking to me?" I ask.

He shrugs again. "I don't know. Elena and Miles were mad that you weren't more careful, and I went along with them because it was easier." He pauses and clears his throat. "Sorry. That wasn't cool."

"Thanks for saying that. I want to fix this somehow. Maybe there's a way to get the Hideout back."

"That would be great," Oliver says. "I miss"—he peeks over his shoulder into the apartment and lowers his voice—"drawing down there."

"I'm going to figure something out," I say, and I mean it. "After we find Ziggy. First I have to get him home to Mae."

Oliver looks down at the search party flyer in his hand. "See you then."

We exchange small smiles and say goodbye.

I'm glad to have one friend back, but now I'm even more nervous about going to see Elena and Miles. What if they refuse to open the door, or slam it in my face?

I take the stairs up the two flights to the fourth floor and ring Elena's doorbell. I force myself to take a deep breath so I won't pass out.

Her brother opens the door. I'm not sure if it's Ethan or Elliot, since they look so similar.

"You're the girl who got caught in the Hideout," he says instead of a hello. My face gets hot.

Then he turns around and yells, "Elena! Your friend is here!"

Elena comes to the door, and as soon as she sees me, I can tell from the expression on her face that she was expecting it to be one of the other kids.

"What are you doing here?" It's the exact same thing Oliver asked, but the way she says it, she sounds less surprised and more annoyed.

"I wanted to give you this." I hand her the flyer and explain about the search party. "I hope you can come."

"I'll let you know," Elena says coldly, and then starts to close the door.

"Wait," I say. "I also wanted to tell you that I'm sorry about everything. I know how much the Hideout meant to you. I didn't mean for any of this to happen. You have to believe me."

"I believe that you didn't mean for it to happen," she says. "But it happened. Because you weren't careful. I don't know why you thought it would be a good idea to fall asleep down there."

"It was a huge mistake," I say. "But I'm going to fix it.

I'm going to find a way to get the Hideout back."

"How?"

"You'll see," I say, since that sounds better than the truth, which is that I have no idea.

"Anyway, see you," I say.

"Bye," Elena says before closing the door.

I head up to the fifth floor next, to see Miles. But when I knock on his door, his mom opens and says that he's in the shower. I give her the flyer to give to him. I think he'll show up to the search party, since he likes Ziggy and Mae, too.

This is the same floor that Nora lives on, so I'm tempted to ring her doorbell. But instead, I slip one of the flyers under her door.

Back in my apartment, I make another mental list. This time, it's a list of wishes.

I wish for Nora to come to the search party.

I wish for Ziggy's safe return.

And I wish for things to get back to the way they were before I messed everything up.

Chapter Thirty

My first wish doesn't come true.

I'm standing in front of twenty or so people in the lobby. It's a pretty good turnout, especially since this search party came together last minute. But the one person I really wanted to come isn't here. I guess I shouldn't be surprised, since Nora's still mad at me. But I thought she'd want to help find Ziggy.

My hands are clammy because I don't love having to speak in front of a group of people, especially so many adults. Besides my parents, there's Carlos and Daniela. Oliver, Elena, and Miles came, along with a couple of their parents. Mae is here, too. She's not going to help us search since her knee is still healing, but she came down-stairs for support. And then there are some neighbors I haven't met before, or have only seen around the build-ing a few times. Like Mr. Hollins.

I take a deep breath and remind myself why I'm here.

"Thanks for coming," I begin, but everyone is still mingling and can't hear me. "Uh, excuse me!" I say louder.

The crowd notices me and gets quiet. Malia moves to the front of it and gives me two thumbs up.

I flash a nervous smile. "Thanks for being here. I was thinking we should break into groups of four or five peo-ple." To get ready for this search, I printed a few copies of a map of our area. On each map, I colored over a differ-ent set of streets in the neighborhood with a highlighter. "Each group should take a map and search the streets that I highlighted. Since there are a lot of apartment buildings on our block, maybe you can try to stop people as they walk in or out. You can also ring their buzzers and ask over the intercom."

"There are some houses on the side streets around here," Dad adds. "So we should knock on those doors, too."

I nod and point to the coffee table in between the couches, where I put out some supplies. "Everyone should carry some flyers with Ziggy's picture, and I also made baggies with Ziggy's favorite dog treats." Last night I did some more research on finding dogs, and read about carrying treats. If Ziggy smells them, he might come out from wherever he's hiding—if he's hiding somewhere. "My dad's cell phone number is on each map, so if you find Ziggy or learn anything helpful, you can call him."

I glance at my phone. "How about we meet back here in an hour? That should be enough time to cover our areas. And pizza will be here when we get back."

Everyone nods.

"Mae?" I ask her in a lower voice. "Do you want to, um, say anything?"

Everyone turns to Mae, who's sitting on one of the armchairs, with her cane leaning against it.

"Just my thanks. Ziggy is everything to me. The thought of losing him forever . . ." Her voice breaks, and she shakes her head sadly. "I appreciate all of you so much for taking the time to look for him."

"We're going to find him," I tell her. *We have to.* To the rest of the room, I say, "Let's start searching!"

Oliver and Miles move next to me. Behind them, Elena is looking at the maps on the coffee table.

"It's so cool that you organized this," Miles says.

"Thanks," I say. "Do you . . . want to be in a group together?"

Miles nods, and Oliver says, "Sure."

"Great." I smile, relieved they are willing to hang out with me again. I wonder if Elena will want to come with us.

Now she's holding a map and a bag of treats. She walks over. "Ready to go?"

She smiles at all of us, even me, and I exhale.

We all head out with my dad. Our map has the streets to the right of our building highlighted, so we walk to the right, which is also toward the park. I keep trying to think like a dog. Where would Ziggy go? During the rain, I'm guessing he looked for a dry place to hide. But then once it ended, maybe he tried to walk back home, but got confused. Or someone saw him wandering around and picked him up.

Between our apartment building and the park entrance are two more buildings, so we stand in front of them for ten minutes to talk to the residents coming in and out. But nobody we talk to has seen Ziggy. After ringing all the buzzers and talking to a few people over the intercom, we decide to keep walking down our street. We'll circle back to the buildings, in case more people show up.

We search and talk to people for another hour, but nobody has seen him anywhere.

I hope one of the other groups had better luck. But if someone had found Ziggy, they would've called Dad.

A couple of the other groups are back inside the lobby when we get there. From the disappointment on their faces, I know they didn't have any luck either. Dad goes over to talk to them and find out more.

We wait for the other groups to return, and then the pizza arrives. Everyone starts eating it, but the mood in the room is grim.

"This is hopeless," I say out loud, to nobody.

Daniela must've heard me, because she comes over and puts her arm around my shoulders. "Don't worry, Joy. I bet you Ziggy is fine. You know, dogs are resourceful animals. They always manage to find a safe space when they need one. He'll turn up. We'll keep searching."

"Thanks," I tell her. I want to believe her, but it's so hard to stay positive.

But then something she said lingers in my brain.

I have an idea.

"Excuse me, I have to check something." Before Daniela can say anything else, I turn around and run.

Chapter Thirty-One

I haven't been inside the storage closet since that morning Mom tracked me down here. I go in, and the shame from betraying the secrecy of the Hideout fills me up again. But something in my gut is telling me to check the place now.

The Hideout was my safe space when I needed it. What if, somehow, it's been Ziggy's safe space all this time, too?

I go to the back of the closet and find the door in the floor. But then I remember that Carlos put a new lock on it, and I don't have the key. I crouch down on the floor and place my ear against the door, hoping I can hear something on the other side. Ziggy whimpering, the jingle of his collar, or any other doggy sounds. But I can't hear anything.

I stand up and rush back out into the hallway and to the lobby, where some people are still hanging around eating pizza.

"Carlos!" I shout. "Where's Carlos?"

"What's going on?" Mom asks.

"I'm here," Carlos says from one of the couches. He's holding a slice of pepperoni pizza.

"Can I borrow the key to the Hideout—the room below the storage closet?" I ask. "For a second? I need to see something."

Dad moves to stand next to me. "The Hideout? You know it's off-limits."

"I know, but I need to see something. I think Ziggy might be down there."

Everyone's looking at me now, confused.

"What?" Mom asks. "How would he have gotten down there?"

"It's a gut feeling." I look at Carlos again. "Please, can I check? You can come with me."

"All right, but I'll be the one to go down there," Carlos says. "In case it's not safe."

"Deal."

I follow Carlos toward the storage closet, and Elena,

Miles, and Oliver are right behind.

"Uh-uh," I hear Miles's mom say. "You aren't going down there."

"I'm not," Miles says.

We all stand in the hallway while Carlos goes inside the closet. I peer in as he disappears around the corner where the Hideout entrance is.

I guess everyone's curious, because soon the whole hallway is full of the people from our search party. Even Mae, who's leaning against another neighbor for support. Everyone gets quiet as they wait to see what will happen next.

I hope my instinct is right and I'm not getting anyone's hopes up.

There's the sound of keys jangling on a key ring, and then a lock opening. The Hideout door makes a familiar creak, and then a light bang as it hits the wall. Then there are footsteps while Carlos walks down the stairs.

My heart beats so fast and loud, it's like I won't be able to hear anything else.

But then there's a bark. It's not very loud, but I definitely hear it.

And then I hear it again.

Carlos says, "¡Dios mío! Ziggy?"

I don't care what my parents say. I immediately run to the back of the closet and down the stairs.

There is Ziggy, laying down on a beanbag chair next to the bookshelf. He looks weak, and like he can't get up. His harness and leash are still on.

"Oh my gosh, Ziggy!" I sit next to him. I almost burst into tears from how happy I am to see him.

"I think he's hurt," Carlos says. "And he's probably dehydrated. I'll go get some water and tell Mae we found him."

I still have a baggie of dog treats in my pocket, so I take it out. I hold a treat out to him and he immediately eats it, and then licks my hand. I give him the rest. "I can't believe I was right. How did you get down here?"

I look around and see the open window at the top of the wall. It's right above the bookshelf. He must've climbed in that way, and then maybe he jumped onto the beanbag chair. Maybe that's how he hurt himself.

But why would he come in this way? Why not wait by the front door for someone to let him in? I try to think of some reasons. Maybe he didn't make it back here until it was late, when nobody was around. Could he have been here since the night he was lost?

"I wish you could tell me what you went through," I

tell Ziggy as I gently rub his head. I'll never know the full story of how he got down here, but I'm so glad he's here and he's safe.

A minute later, Carlos is back with water, and my dad is right behind him.

"Wow," he says when he sees Ziggy.

"I think he climbed in through that window," I say. "He found his way home after all."

"He needs to see a vet," Dad says, concern written all over his face. "Is there something we can use as a small stretcher? I don't want to hurt him worse by carrying him upstairs myself."

"I'll go find something," Carlos says.

While he goes, I open the bottle of water Carlos brought down and slowly pour some out near Ziggy's mouth so he can lick it up. He drinks half the bottle.

Carlos comes back with a laundry basket and towel. He puts the towel in the basket and places it on the floor. "It was the only thing I could think of. Let's move him into this and bring him upstairs. Mae can't wait to see him."

Dad carefully lifts Ziggy. He whimpers at first, but once he's in the basket, he stops. Then Carlos lifts the laundry basket and carries it upstairs.

As soon as everyone sees Carlos walk out of the closet

with Ziggy, they cheer. They give him space as he walks Ziggy out into the lobby, where Mae is sitting on a couch. He puts the basket next to her, and Ziggy tries to jump out of it to greet her. But then he yelps in pain and lays back down.

"Oh, Ziggy, my poor baby." Mae takes Ziggy's face in her hands and leans over to rest her head against his. Ziggy licks her hand over and over as she pets him. When Mae sits up again, she wipes a tear from her eye. "I'm so glad you're okay. We're going to get you checked out, all right? You're safe now."

The whole room is quiet. Watching Mae and Ziggy reunite is the best feeling ever.

"Thank you, Joy," Mae says, and my whole body gets warm.

The only thing that would make this moment more perfect is if Nora were here to share it with me.

Mae calls her vet to see if she can get an emergency appointment to have Ziggy checked out. Meanwhile, everyone else either heads home or goes back to eating pizza and talking. The mood is much happier now that Ziggy is here.

I go over to where Miles, Oliver, and Elena are standing.

"Thanks for coming today," I say.

"I can't believe Ziggy was down in the Hideout," Miles says before taking a huge bite of cheese pizza.

"Seriously," Elena says. "To think that if we were still hanging out down there, we would've found him sooner."

Her words are a slap in the face.

"Sorry," Elena says quickly. "I didn't mean . . . I mean, I forgive you."

"It's fine," I say.

"Ziggy's safe now," Oliver says. "That's what matters."

"Right," Elena says. "By the way, where's Nora? She should be here, too."

"Yeah, where is she?" Oliver repeats.

"I invited her," I say. "But we sort of got into a fight before Ziggy got lost. She's mad at me."

"That stinks," Miles says.

"But you're right," I say. "Someone should tell her that Ziggy is safe. I'll be right back."

This could be my chance to get Nora to talk to me again, so we can fix our friendship.

I ask Mom if it's okay if I run up to Nora's apartment to tell her, and she says it's fine. I take the elevator up and knock on Nora's door. My mind races as I try to think of what to say if she answers.

A minute later, Felix opens the door. "Hi, Joy," he says.

"Hi. Can I speak to Nora?"

"Come on in." He steps to the side so I can walk into the apartment. "She's in her room, so I'll go check with her." Normally, he'd tell me to go straight back to her room, so he must know about our fight.

I stand by the door, rocking back and forth on my heels as I wait.

A minute later, Felix comes back out.

"I'm sorry," he says. "Nora's tired and doesn't want to talk right now."

"Oh, okay." All the excitement about finding Ziggy is replaced with dread. "Can you tell her that we found Ziggy? He's okay."

"That's great news," Felix says. "I'm sure Nora will be thrilled to hear that."

Just not thrilled to hear that I stopped by.

I say goodbye and head back downstairs, where my parents and everyone are still eating pizza.

"You tell her?" Miles asks when he sees that I'm back.

"Um, she was busy, so I told her dad," I say.

"Cool."

"I need pizza." I grab a slice and take a bite. But the lump in my throat makes it hard to swallow.

That night when I'm getting ready for bed, I think about Nora again. I need to convince her to talk to me. I could make a long list of all the things I miss about her. Like talking about our favorite movies, and exploring the building, and taking walks in the park, with or without the dogs. I miss having her as a friend. I let her down, and I'm desperate to make it up to her.

But how? I think about everything I know about her. What matters the most to her? Her family and her screenplay. I'd told her that I would help her with her music score, but the music usually comes after the filming, and she hasn't done that yet. Plus, I still need to learn how to play the piano.

I think some more about everything Nora and I have talked about, and the solution is obvious. There's one thing that Nora, and our other friends, want back. One thing that will make all of us happy again.

The Hideout.

Chapter Thirty-Two

If my plan is going to work, I need Elena, Miles, and Oliver to help. Mom lets me have my phone back for good, so I send them a group text on Sunday morning.

ME: I want to figure out how to get the Hideout back. Can you meet up at 4?

It only takes a few seconds for the first text to appear.

MILES: I'm in! Where?
OLIVER: Me too
ELENA: 👍

ME: Yay!

ME: Let's meet . . .

I stop typing. Where should we meet? Normally I'd say the Hideout because it's the one place in the building where we could be alone. Then I think of someplace else.

ME: Let's meet in the basement by the trash chute

I tell my mom that I'm meeting up with the other kids downstairs and will be back in an hour.

But before I take the elevator to the basement, I go next door to check on Mae and Ziggy.

"Hi, Joy," Mae says when she opens the door. She looks happier than I've seen her in a while.

"I came to see how Ziggy's doing," I say. "After his vet appointment."

"Come in and see for yourself."

She turns around, walking carefully with her cane. I close her front door and follow her.

She leads me into her bedroom, where Ziggy is laying on her bed, surrounded by pillows. He's asleep, so I stand at the doorway so I won't disturb him. His back leg is wrapped up and he's wearing a fabric cone around his neck. It's yellow, and it makes Ziggy look like a sunflower. I smile.

"The vet gave him painkillers, so he's a little drowsy," Mae says in a low voice. "The good news is he didn't break his leg. It's only a fracture. The vet says he should be back to running around like normal soon enough."

"That's great."

"I got him a fabric cone so he can be more comfortable. Plus, it's cute." She laughs quietly. "I really missed him."

"I know," I say. "I'm so glad he's home."

"The vet said he was quite dehydrated. I'm not sure how much longer he could've survived down in that room. I'm so glad you thought to check there."

"Me too. Can I come by again when he's awake?"

Mae gives a warm smile. "Anytime."

I say goodbye and head down to the basement. The other kids will be there soon.

As I'm about to walk from the elevator to the trash chute room at the other end of the hall, I notice the door to another room. I peek inside. Natural light comes through a tall window and shows a dusty room full of random junk: boxes, discarded furniture, metal folding chairs. It's nothing special, just a regular basement room. I turn off the light and leave.

The elevator dings, and out walk Miles, Oliver, and Elena.

"We all got in the same elevator," Oliver explains.

I smile. "Follow me." I lead them down the hall to the room where Nora and I talked to Carlos that time he was fixing the trash chute.

Elena looks around and pinches her nose. "Why'd you pick this place? It almost smells as bad as my brothers' room after soccer practice."

"Because we can be alone here," I say.

"Can we open this door?" Oliver walks up to the door that leads to outside. It has a small glass window.

"We probably shouldn't," I say. "I'll make this quick. We want to use the Hideout again, right? Even if it's not a secret anymore, we should try to convince our parents to let us hang out there. So we can still have a place to go when we need our own space."

"How will we convince them?" Miles asks.

"That's what we need to figure out," I say. "When Nora and I wanted to walk dogs, we got our parents together and shared a presentation with reasons why we thought they should give us permission. Maybe we could do something like that."

"Know what I think?" Oliver asks. "We have to talk to Carlos first. He's the one with the key. If he says it's okay to be down there, that would help us convince our parents that it's okay, too."

"You're right," I say. "Let's go talk to Carlos."

"Now?" Miles asks.

"What do you think, Elena?" I ask, noticing she hasn't said anything since complaining about the smell.

"Anything to get away from this trash. I hope the smell isn't sticking to me." I can tell she's not breathing through her nose.

I laugh. "Let's go see if he's home."

A minute later, Carlos greets us at his door.

"We want to talk to you about the Hideout," I say.

His eyebrows wrinkle. "The Hideout?"

"Yeah, the room where we found Ziggy," I say.

"Ah, yes."

"How can we convince you to open it up and let us hang out there again?" Miles asks. Straight to the point. I like his style.

Carlos frowns. "Well, I'm sorry, but that's not going to happen."

"Why not?" Elena asks. "I promise, we weren't doing anything bad down there. We were playing games and stuff."

"And we can stop drawing on the walls," Oliver says, even though I can tell he doesn't want to.

"Yeah, if you want us to paint over that, we can," I add.

"It's not that," Carlos says. "It's about safety. That

room—I talked to the building owner about it, and even she didn't know about it. She only bought the property eight years ago, though, and I've only been here for five years. Anyway, the room isn't up to code."

"What's that mean?" Miles asks.

"There are certain requirements for spaces in an apartment building," Carlos explains. "If that room is only being used for storage, then nothing needs to be done. But if you want to spend time down there, it needs to have an exit to outside. In case of a fire. The stairs leading back into the closet aren't enough."

"But there's a window," I say. "Ziggy got in that way."

"Right, but that window is small," Carlos says. "It was fine for Ziggy to fit through, and maybe a small child, but not big kids like you. Or an adult, if someone needed to come rescue you in an emergency. I'm glad nothing bad happened when you were down there."

"Can't you install a larger window?" Miles asks.

"I wish I could, but it's up to the owner. And those upgrades cost money."

"How much money?" I ask, thinking of my dog-walking earnings. It's not a lot, but maybe I could contribute.

"I don't know exactly, but my guess is at least a thousand dollars—between the materials and the labor. Maybe more."

"Dang, that's a lot of money." Miles says what we're all thinking.

"The owner's not going to pay for that," Carlos says. "She's conservative with her spending, and usually only wants to pay for repairs and such. It took her a while to finally renovate the lobby. I'm sorry. My hands are tied."

Next to me, Elena sighs. "Thanks anyway."

We say goodbye and go into the lobby.

Oliver collapses onto one of the couches. "It was worth a shot."

Elena sits next to him. "Yeah, at least we tried."

I'm too antsy to sit. "No," I say. "I'm not giving up yet."

"You heard Carlos," Miles says. "The owner won't pay."

"I know. It's just, there's got to be some other way," I say.

"I know you feel guilty about what happened, and we were pretty terrible to you. I admit that," Elena says. "But we'll still be your friend even if we don't get the Hideout back."

"I know," I say.

But will Nora be my friend again?

"I should probably head home," Miles says.

"Me too," Oliver says.

"Same," Elena says. "But if you come up with any other ideas, keep us posted."

"Thanks, guys," I say.

I need to think. This was only the first part of my plan to save my friendship with Nora, and already I've hit a huge hurdle. I'm angry at myself all over again for leading my mom to the Hideout in the first place. It was the one place in this building where I felt at home.

The Hideout was there when I needed to get away from my parents' arguments. When I needed a place to be alone. It was the place where I could have fun with my new friends. And the place where I could write notes and open up to . . . Nora.

It was our secret refuge.

And now it's really gone. Forever.

An idea comes to me in the middle of the night. It's like my brain was figuring it out, putting the pieces together while I was in a deep sleep, and once it's fully formed, it wakes me up.

I might have the answer to winning back Nora's friendship.

Chapter Thirty-Three

I get ready faster than normal so I can talk to Carlos before school. But first I go back down to the basement to look at the room next to the elevator again. The one that's full of junk.

What if it could be a *new* Hideout?

The basement is empty, like the other times I was here. It seems like nobody comes down here, except for Carlos sometimes. It makes this room even more perfect. The other kids and I could still come down here when we want to hang out without our parents around. Nobody would bother us.

I turn on the lights and look around the room. I don't

know for sure that the bigger window means it's up to code or whatever, but Carlos would know. Then if we got permission from the owner to use the space, we could fix it up. My mom could help—she watches so much HGTV, she'd know exactly what to do. Then my friends and I would have a new safe space to hang out in together.

I try to imagine it with all of the boxes and junk gone, and set up like the Hideout. It's got even more space for our bookshelf, rug, and beanbag chairs. It's kind of a dusty mess right now, but so are a lot of the "before" rooms on the home improvement shows Mom watches. Excitement bubbles up inside me as I realize that this could actually work.

But only if Carlos and the building owner agree to it.

"Good morning, Joy," Carlos says as he opens his door.

I don't have a second to waste, so I get straight to the point, like Miles did last night. "Morning. I want to ask you about the empty room down in the basement, right near the elevator. I saw some old furniture in there. Is it being used for storage or something?" I ask.

Carlos's forehead wrinkles. "Not officially. A lot of that junk needs to go in the trash. Some of it was stuff from before we renovated the lobby."

This was great news. "If nobody's using the room for anything, do you think it could be made into a new space for kids to hang out in? It has a bigger window, so that means it's safe, right?"

"The basement rooms are up to code, yes," Carlos says. "But, like I said before, I'm not sure the owner would want to pay to fix it up."

"What if my parents and friends helped clean it out? I could pay for the paint and supplies with my dog-walking money. If you don't need it, we could even reuse some of the furniture that's in there. Then this project wouldn't cost the owner anything."

Carlos looks at me with a curious expression. "Why are you so interested in doing this? Does it have anything to do with why I haven't seen you and Nora together lately?"

"Something like that," I say. "Please? This is really important to me."

"Well, I'd still have to get the owner's approval," Carlos says. "But I'll let her know that she won't have to pay for the paint or anything. That could be enough to convince her."

"Thank you so much!"

Carlos smiles. "You're welcome. You're a good friend."

"I'm trying," I say. "You'll tell me as soon as you hear back from the owner?"

"You'll know as soon as I hear something."

I head outside with a huge smile on my face. But when I get close to the bus stop, I freeze. Elena, Miles, Oliver, and Nora are standing together, like normal. I'm dying to go over there and tell Elena, Miles, and Oliver about my new plan, but I can't tell them in front of Nora. Not to mention Nora still doesn't want anything to do with me, so how can I go over there at all? I guess I'm stuck standing halfway down the block, alone, again.

I sit on the curb and take out my headphones. The first song that comes up on my movie score playlist is from *Jurassic Park*. The same song I was listening to that first time I talked to Nora in the elevator.

As I listen, I try to think positive thoughts. My new plan will work. Nora and I will be friends again. And soon, I'll get to hang out with all of my friends at the bus stop—and in the new Hideout. Until then, I have to be patient—and strong.

After school, I take the manila envelope out of my desk drawer, and count my dog-walking money. I have a hundred and ten dollars, which isn't that much, but it'll have to work. The main thing we'll need is paint, since we can reuse the other stuff from the original Hideout.

I open the Notes app on my phone and create a new list:

Basement Room Makeover

○ Get rid of the junk and furniture we won't need
○ Clean up and get rid of all dust
○ Paint the walls
○ Move everything over from original Hideout

I'm glad the last day of school is this week, so I won't have anything else to distract me.

That night, while I'm eating dinner with Mom and Malia, there's a knock on our door.

"I'll get it," I say. When I look through the peep hole, Carlos is on the other side.

"Hi, Joy," Carlos says when I open the door. He waves to my mom and Malia. "Sorry to interrupt your dinner— is that curry? It smells great."

"Hi, Carlos," Mom says. "What brings you here?"

"I came to give Joy some news," Carlos says. "The owner agreed to let you fix up the room, as long as she doesn't have to spend any extra money."

"Oh my gosh, that's amazing!" I say. "Thank you!"

"No problem." Carlos grins. "Let me know how I can help."

"Can you get rid of the stuff we won't need down there?" I ask.

"Sure. I'll move the boxes to a storage closet. And I'll

look into whether a donation company can pick up the rest."

When I get back to my seat at the table, Mom asks, "What was that about?"

"I know we can't have the Hideout back, and that lying to our parents about where we were was wrong," I say. "But I was thinking, what if there was another space in the building where we could hang out? A space that all the parents know about, but it'll still be for just us kids." I explain how I found the room in the basement, and how Carlos said it wasn't being used for anything.

"Interesting," Mom says.

"Is that okay with you?" I ask.

"I mean, if it's in the building and I know where you'll be, then I guess that's okay," Mom says.

I grin.

"Can I go, too?" Malia asks.

"When you're older," I say. "It's going to be a space for the older kids to hang out."

"That's not fair and you know it!" Malia crosses her arms.

"It's all the way in the basement," I tell her. "There might even be spiders down there."

Her eyes get wide. "Spiders? Actually, never mind."

I turn to Mom. "Will you help me with fixing up the

room? You're so good at interior design stuff."

Mom's face lights up. "I'd love to help."

"There's one condition. I'm paying for the paint supplies and stuff with my dog-walking money."

"Are you sure? You're supposed to use that money for yourself."

"I know," I say. "But I want to do this."

After dinner, I text Elena, Miles, and Oliver and explain everything. I ask if they can help clean up and paint the basement room over the next few days. They immediately text back and agree.

Hideout #2 is officially underway.

Chapter Thirty-Four

The last day of school means one thing: Dairy Queen. It's our tradition with Dad. I get a Reese's Peanut Butter Cup Blizzard, Malia gets a cookie dough Blizzard, and Dad gets a chocolate-dipped cone.

It's crowded—other families had the same idea—but we find an empty bench in the shade.

"Your mom told me about the room in the basement that you're fixing up," Dad says.

"She told you?" I ask.

"Yeah," Dad says. "You're surprised?"

I shrug. "I thought you weren't talking that much anymore."

"You're not talking to Mommy?" Malia asks.

"We're still talking," Dad says. "We're still married, and we plan to stay that way."

That makes Malia smile.

Then why are you still living at Uncle Spencer's house? I want to ask, but don't. Now isn't the time.

"Can you take me somewhere after we finish our ice cream?" I ask. "It's for the room."

"Where?"

"The thrift store."

"Sure."

After ice cream, Dad takes us to the same thrift store where I saw the piano over a month ago. I'm surprised to see that it's still for sale when I walk in. But this time, I ignore the piano and walk to the back corner of the store. I'm looking for something that I remember seeing the last time I was here. Something for the new Hideout.

When I finally spot it, I'm relieved. It's still here. I'm so happy nobody bought it! The sticker says it's forty dollars. Dad helps me pick up the box and carry it to the register.

"Don't forget to bargain," Dad says. "You might be able to get it for thirty bucks instead."

"Okay," I say.

At the register is an older man reading a newspaper. He puts it down when he sees us.

"I'd like to buy this, please," I say.

"Forty dollars," he says, glancing at the tag.

"How about thirty?" I ask him.

The man narrows his eyes at me. "Thirty-eight."

"Thirty-five," I counteroffer.

"Fine," he says, and rings it up on the register.

I smile at Dad, who winks at me.

I hand over thirty-five dollars, and Dad helps me carry it to the car.

"Is that for our room?" Malia asks as Dad loads the box into the trunk.

"No, it's for the basement room I'm fixing up."

"The one with the spiders?"

"Yup."

Malia shudders.

After Mom gets home from work, Dad stays with Malia for a little longer so Mom and I can go down to the room in the basement. I want to figure out what furniture we should keep, before Carlos schedules a donation company to come by for the rest.

When I turn the light on in the room, I start to second guess myself. It needs a lot of work. It's so dirty down here. I was kidding with Malia before about the spiders, but there probably *are* spiderwebs everywhere. This room is a far cry from the kind of space the other kids—and

Nora—would want to hang out in. Why did I think I could make this room into something nice?

But then Mom says, "This space has a ton of potential." She has the biggest smile on her face, and it's like her HGTV-loving dreams are coming true.

"You honestly think we can make this work?" I ask.

"Once we clear everything out and clean the floors, you'll see. We'll add fresh paint to these walls, and it'll look good as new. For now, let's decide what furniture we should keep and what we should let Carlos give away."

"Let me take a 'before' picture first." I stand in the doorway and snap a picture of the room in all of its cluttered, dusty glory.

Mom sees the expression on my face as I'm reviewing the photo I took. "It's going to look great by the time we're done. Don't worry."

On Thursday, Mom goes to work as usual and Dad comes over. He stays in our apartment with Malia while I meet Elena, Miles, and Oliver in the basement.

Carlos also comes by to help. "The donation place can't pick up the furniture until next week," he says. "But in the meantime, we can move it into the hallway."

Together, we move everything out. All that's left when we're done is a black couch, coffee table, two side tables, a folding table and chairs, plus a couple of lamps. It all looks kind of boring, since it's old lobby furniture. But it's more than we ever had in the original Hideout.

We just have to make it our own. Mom says we can sand down and repaint the side tables a fun color. We can add a colorful throw blanket to the couch. And the lamps will make the space much cozier than the overhead fluorescent lights.

"It's so cool that we'll have an actual couch now," Elena says.

"I still like the beanbag chairs, though," Oliver says. "We should bring those in here."

"Definitely," I say. The beanbag chairs come with a lot of memories. Like when I wrote those messages to Nora on the wall, when we sat on them during game night, and when I fell asleep on one of them. They're part of the Hideout's history. And part of my history in this building.

"Hey, I was thinking," I say. "We should each have a space to do our favorite things down here. Like, Oliver, we should make sure you have an area to do your art."

Oliver smiles. "I don't need much, just a comfy place to sit. But maybe I'll bring my drawing supplies down here."

"Good idea," Elena says. "I could bring down my sewing machine! I'm learning how to sew so I can make my own LARP costumes and stuff."

"You can put it on the card table," I suggest.

"Yeah, and I'll store it on the bookshelf when I'm not using it."

"That's perfect." I turn to Miles. "How about you?"

He shrugs. "I'm just excited to come down here to hang out with you all. But I'll bring some of my favorite books, too. Maybe we can start a library."

"The beanbag chairs are really comfy for reading," I say. "Just don't fall asleep on them for too long." I laugh.

"What about you, Joy?" Elena asks.

I think about what I bought at the thrift store. If everything works out, pretty soon I'll have an exciting project to work on.

"I'll practice my music stuff," I say. *And prepare to become the next big film composer.*

"Sounds like a plan," Elena says.

Before we can arrange the room and create our own spaces, we have to clean it from top to bottom. We spend the rest of the day de-dustifying—my term for getting rid of all of the icky dust—and mopping the floors. We wipe down the baseboards and the light covers on the ceiling. Carlos lends us a ladder for that part. I end up seeing lots of spiderwebs, but thankfully no actual spiders.

By the time Mom gets home from work, the room is cleared out and sparkling clean. The next step is to paint, but before we can do that, we have to buy all of the supplies. The other kids head home while Mom takes me to the store before dinner.

"I want to paint one wall white," I say. "It's for a surprise."

"Okay, what about the other walls?" Mom asks. "Do you have another color in mind?"

"I'm not sure."

Mom leads us to the paint department. "Since the basement doesn't get as much light as upstairs, we should stick to lighter colors."

As we stare at the wall of paint swatches, I try to think of what color Nora would like. I don't actually know her favorite color. But I know she loves the Mets, and their team colors are navy and orange. Orange isn't right for the space, and navy would be too dark, but a lighter blue could work.

"How about blue?" I ask.

"Good choice," Mom says. "Most people like blue." We look through paint swatches until we find a turquoise color called Florida Keys Blue. It'll go well with the gray tile that's already on the floor in the room.

I use the rest of my dog-walking money to buy a couple of gallons of the blue paint, as well as a gallon of white paint, and several paint rollers and trays. We also buy supplies to repaint the side tables yellow. Mom pitches in some of her own money when I realize I don't have enough.

"It's a gift, for all your hard work," she says.

After dinner, Mom and I get to work on the side tables. Watching all those makeover shows has paid off, because Mom knows exactly what to do. I turn on my movie score playlist, and we sand them down, paint primer on them, and then add a coat of the yellow paint. It's really nice to work on this project together.

Then, bright and early on Friday morning, Miles, Oliver, Elena, and I paint the walls. We're dressed in clothes we don't care about, and I wrap my hair in an old scarf so paint won't get in it. I bring down speakers and play upbeat music while we work. It's a lot more fun than cleaning. By the time we're done putting up two coats of paint, the room looks amazing, like so much more than a basement storage room. I also add another coat of paint to the yellow side tables. They look so cheery.

When there's nothing left to paint, Carlos helps us bring over the stuff from the original Hideout, so we can set up the rest of the room. We hang the fabric mural on one of the blue walls, and the Christmas lights across the ceiling. We place the rug on the floor, set up the card table, position the bookshelf, and find the best spot for the beanbag chairs.

Mom also suggests that I take pictures of the wall that kids drew and wrote on in the original Hideout. She offers to help us frame them, so we can hang them up in the new space later on. It's such a great idea. Carlos lets me in, and I get some close-up shots and some from far away. I also take some pictures of Nora's poem and our back-and-forth messages below it, for myself.

It's strange to think that no other kid will get to come down to this room anymore, but I like knowing that I got to leave my stamp on it. And now I'll have these pictures to look back on.

The only thing left to do in the Hideout is set up my thrift store purchase. Carlos helps me with that, and it looks exactly like I imagined.

And then we're done. We're sweaty and covered in paint splatter, but we did it. We created our new Hideout.

"It looks so good!" Elena says. "I already can't wait for our next game night."

"I can't wait to come draw down here," Oliver says.

"It's so much better than the old Hideout," Miles says.

"I couldn't have done it without your help," I say.

I take out my phone and snap an "after" photo of the room. Next to the "before" photo, the room looks completely transformed. I can't believe we pulled this off.

All I need to do now is get Nora to come down to the basement for the big reveal.

And I know exactly how I'm going to do it.

Chapter Thirty-Five

First, I go to my apartment to take a quick shower and change my clothes, so Nora doesn't see paint splatter on me. Then I take the elevator up to her floor, my nerves multiplying every second. What if this doesn't work?

I take a deep breath and ring her doorbell. This is it.

When Nora opens the door, she looks surprised to see me standing here. Then she sees the expression on my face. "What's wrong?"

"Nora, you have to come with me." I make my voice sound panicked. "It's Tank. Something happened downstairs. I need your help!"

"What?" Now she looks worried. "Oh no! What happened to Tank?"

"Just come with me." I turn and walk to the elevator, hoping she'll trust me and follow.

She yells from behind me, "Dad, I'm going with Joy for a minute. Be right back!" and then runs into the open elevator, where I'm waiting.

"Is Tank hurt? What's going on?" Nora asks as I press the button for the basement.

She notices that and asks, "Why are we going to the basement?"

"You'll understand when we get there," is all I say, which only makes Nora look even more confused.

The elevator starts moving, and I stare at the numbers going down. I hope this works, and that it's enough to get Nora to forgive me.

"Where are you taking me?"

Ignoring her, I lead her into the brand-new Hideout.

I stand to the side as Nora freezes and looks around the room, completely confused. "What . . . what is all this? Where's Tank?"

"Tank's fine," I say. "He's home. I just said that to get you down here."

She looks around the room—at the fresh paint on the walls, the shiny tile floor covered with our rug from the

Hideout, the furniture, some of it familiar and some not. And then her eyes land on my surprise—a projector in the middle of the room, with a big red bow around it. The four folding chairs are behind it. And on the white painted wall across from it, it projects the phrase, "A Short Film by Nora Ramos, coming soon."

Nora looks at me like she's at a loss for words.

"It's for when your movie is done," I say. "You can debut it down here for our friends. We can even get dressed up and create a red carpet. And of course, I'll help you with the movie score . . . if you still want me to."

"You did this for me?" she asks.

I grin. "Yup."

"What is this place?"

"It's our new Hideout," I say.

"Seriously?"

I nod. "Carlos says we can hang out down here now since the old Hideout isn't safe." I explain how Elena, Miles, Oliver, and I spent the week fixing it up.

"Wow." Nora walks around the room and takes it all in.

"What do you think?" I ask. "I wanted to do something nice for you, because I know that I hurt you, and I'm sorry. I really, really miss you." My eyes get blurry with tears.

"It's . . . amazing." She turns to me, and her eyes are a

little watery, too. "I can't believe you did this."

She goes over to the projector and drags her fingers over it.

"It was wrong of me to expect you to tell me about your problems, just because I told you about mine," I tell her. "From now on—if you'll be my friend again—I promise I'll be there for you, but if you don't want to talk about something, we won't."

"Okay," Nora says.

"Okay what?"

Nora smiles. "I'll be your friend again."

"Really?"

She nods. "I missed you, too. And of course I still want you to help me with my film score."

I go over to her, and we give each other a big hug.

Then I hear clapping coming from the hallway.

We look toward the doorway. Standing there are my mom, Carlos, Elena, Oliver, and Miles, all smiling at us.

"It's great to see you two together again," Carlos says.

Nora and I grin at each other.

"I'm going to head home, but this is your space now," Carlos says. "Make sure to take care of it. And keep it clean."

"We will," I say. "We promise."

Mom says she'll also see me back upstairs.

When the grown-ups are gone, Elena rushes over to me and Nora and wraps her arms around us. "The Fab Five is back!"

"Group hug!" Miles says, slamming us from behind.

Oliver squeezes himself into the hug, too.

My whole body relaxes, and I can't stop smiling.

"Thank you, guys," Nora says. "But, um, you all kind of stink."

We burst out laughing as we separate.

"We didn't want to shower and miss the surprise!" Elena explains. "And then we were waiting by the trash chute while Joy showed you the room." She sniffs herself and wrinkles her nose. "Eww. I'm gonna go shower. Let's finish this reunion tomorrow."

"Yeah, I'm beat," Miles says.

"Game night tomorrow night?" Oliver asks.

We agree to meet up then.

Oliver, Elena, and Miles go out into the hall, and I start to follow them.

"Joy, wait," Nora says. "Can I talk to you for a second?"

"Sure."

We wave goodbye to the others and then I collapse onto the couch. Now that the new Hideout is done, it's hitting me how tired I am. This was a lot of work.

Nora sits next to me. "I just want to say I'm sorry, too. For not admitting I was the one who wrote the poem. I should've just told you."

"It's okay. I understand."

"I hated lying to you about it."

"I'm just glad we're friends again," I say. "I missed being able to talk to you. Especially after I lost Ziggy."

"I'm so sorry about that," Nora says. "I felt super guilty because I knew if I'd been there with you, it probably wouldn't have happened."

"It's in the past now, and Ziggy's safe. His vet says he'll be fine."

"I'm so glad."

"Are you feeling better about . . . you know, what happened with your dad when you got your period?" I ask.

Nora nods. "We talked about it, and he also asked if I wanted to talk to my aunt about it. So I did a video call with her, and she explained a lot to me. That helped."

"Good."

"I still miss my mom a lot. I try not to think about it, but sometimes it just hits me."

"It's okay to miss her," I say. "And it's okay to feel sad."

As soon as the words come out of my mouth, I realize just how true they are—for Nora, and for me too.

It's okay for me to miss my house. It's okay to be sad that my family had to move.

And it's also okay to let myself be happy here.

Nora is quiet for a few moments as she looks around the room. "It's so weird that we can't go back to the other Hideout anymore. So much has changed." She pauses. "Should we come up with a new name for this room? Something other than the Hideout?"

"We probably should," I say. "Especially since we don't have to hide in here anymore. Do you have any ideas?"

"Um . . . the Hangout?" she suggests.

"Fabulous Five's . . . Fortress?" I ask.

"The Cave?"

"Maybe we should sleep on it. And ask the others."

Nora laughs. "Yeah."

Then I ask, "Do you think we'll walk dogs again?"

"I don't know," Nora says. "I still want to save up for my camera. Oh! Speaking of, I finished my script and sent it to Ms. Francis. She's going to email me her comments sometime this summer."

"That's amazing! I can't wait to read it."

Nora grins. "Even if Joyful Dog Walkers doesn't open up again, I'm glad we did it."

"Me too." I lean over to hug her.

"All right," Nora says. "That's enough cheesiness for one night."

I laugh. "There's no such thing."

It's time for both of us to go home. As we wait for the elevator, I give Nora the full recap of how we found Ziggy in the old Hideout.

"Wow, it's like a scene from a movie," she says. "I wish I'd been there."

When we get to my floor and say goodbye, I think about the last wish I made—that everything would get back to the way it was before I messed everything up. It didn't exactly come true, because things aren't like they were before. They're actually better.

Chapter Thirty-Six

Dad comes over the next morning, and at first, it's like old times. He makes pancakes, eggs, and bacon, and then he sits between me and Malia on the couch as we watch cartoons. I'm still tired from all the work I did on the Hideout this week, but it's a good kind of tired.

But then Dad turns off the TV, and Mom comes into the room to sit with us. That's when I realize Dad didn't only come to make breakfast and hang out with us. We're having another family meeting.

Oh no.

"We want to talk to you about something," Mom says.

"Wait," I interrupt, terrified of what she'll say. Dad

already moved out, so what would come next? *Divorce.*

I stand up. "You can't get divorced. I know you're having problems, but you can't. We've already lost our house and gone through so many changes. You need to stay together!" I collapse into the armchair and put my face in my hands.

"What?" Mom and Dad say at the same time.

"You're getting divorced?" Malia asks, her voice trembling.

"No!" Dad says.

I look up at them. Dad has his arm around Malia.

"Honey, we're not getting divorced," Mom tells me.

"You're not?" I ask.

"No," Dad says. "We're seeing a great counselor right now. She's helping us work things out."

"But why haven't you moved back in?" I ask Dad.

Dad glances at Mom and then back at me. "I'm going to. Soon. We didn't want to keep fighting in front of you, so I decided to stay at Spencer's until we finish some more counseling. But we're communicating much better now."

"Really?" The tightness in my chest loosens.

"Really," Dad says.

The relief makes me dizzy.

"I know this has been tough on both of you," Mom

says. "But we're here for you. That's what we wanted to talk about."

Mom moves to kneel in front of me and holds my hands. "I'm sorry for not realizing how much all of this change affected you. I thought you were handling it all pretty well, but when you said you hide your feelings for Malia's sake? That broke my heart. You shouldn't have to do that. You can feel whatever you want, and we'll help. Let us be the strong ones for Malia."

I nod.

"Yes," Dad says. "If there's anything that's bothering you, you can come to us."

"Well," I say. "There is something else that's been bothering me."

"What is it?" Mom asks, moving to sit on the couch next to me.

"I really, really want to take piano lessons," I say. "Like, it's been my dream, and because we don't have any extra money, I won't get to do it. That's why I was walking the dogs, to make some money myself. I thought if I could save up enough for a semester of classes, and maybe buy a used keyboard, you'd let me take lessons. But then that whole plan exploded when I lost Ziggy. And then I used the money I made to fix up the new Hideout. Which I'm glad I did, and it was worth it. But now I'm back at square one, and I still want to learn the piano."

"Oh, honey," Mom says. "I understand. We know how much the piano means to you. And . . . I have some good news."

"What good news?" I ask.

"I was talking to one of our neighbors," Mom says. "Have you met Mr. Hollins?"

The memory of his face when he saw me and Miles in the laundry carts fills my mind.

"Sort of," I say.

"We were in the same group when we were out looking for Ziggy, and I was telling him more about you and Malia. It turns out his wife used to teach piano. She's retired now."

"Okay . . ."

"They still have a piano in their apartment, and Mr. Hollins says you can use it to practice."

I'm shocked. "Really?"

"Yes," Mom says. "He said you can come by any time after school or on the weekends. Mrs. Hollins isn't up to teaching anymore, but he thinks she'd love to hear someone practicing around her again. He's a nice man."

Wow. I guess I had him all wrong. "That's so nice of them. Wait—why didn't you tell me this earlier?"

"I meant to," Mom says, "but then you asked for my help with the basement, and I got caught up in that and forgot to bring it up."

"This is so cool!" I say.

Now I just need to figure out how to learn how to play the piano.

"As for the lessons," Dad says, reading my thoughts. "I can help you with that. I've officially signed on to work with Spencer on his construction company. And we just booked our first big job. It'll take a while for me to make the salary I was making with my old job, but since we're living in this building now, where it's cheaper for us, I can afford your piano lessons."

"For real?" I can't believe what I'm hearing. I also notice how Dad said *we're* living here now. I hope this means he'll move back in sooner rather than later.

"Yes," Dad says. "You deserve it."

"I want you to know," Mom says, "we loved our house, too, and wish we didn't have to sell it. But we did it so you can have a better life in the long run. So we can be financially stable. I still hope to get a promotion at work. And your dad and Spencer have been working really hard on their company."

"You're okay with that now?" I ask Mom. "With Dad working with Uncle Spencer?"

She nods. "We've been talking about this with our

counselor. He and Spencer are excited about it, and it seems to be going well. I was nervous at first, but now I want to be supportive."

"Plus, I get to let my beard grow in again," Dad says with a laugh. He reaches over and squeezes Mom's hand, which makes my own heart squeeze.

"Anyway," Mom continues. "Hopefully in a couple of years we'll be in a better place financially, and we can get you your own piano."

"I can be patient," I say. "Especially with Mr. and Mrs. Hollins being so nice."

"That's great," Dad says. "In the meantime, if you want to walk dogs again with Nora, we can talk about that."

"Maybe just Ziggy, if Mae is open to it." I loved all the dogs, but he's the one I miss seeing every day the most.

"We'll see what Mae thinks when Ziggy's all healed," Mom says.

"You know, I still do miss the house, but this building is growing on me," I say. "Especially the people. If we hadn't moved here, maybe I would've never become friends with Nora, and she's the best. Plus Miles, Oliver, and Elena. I definitely wouldn't have met Mae and Ziggy. Everyone here has been so supportive and nice."

"We're lucky," Mom says.

"I still hate how thin the walls are," I say.

"Me too," Mom says. "But we're working around it."

"And I wish our apartment had a view of the park instead of the street."

"Maybe one day," Dad says.

"But I'm just glad you two aren't getting divorced," I say with a big exhale.

"Me too!" Malia says.

"Nah," Dad says. "Your mom is stuck with me forever."

Mom smiles at him. To me and Malia, she says, "And you're stuck with us. We love you girls so much." She pulls me over to the couch so all four of us are sitting together. Mom and Dad wrap their arms around both of us.

And then it hits me, like a puzzle coming together in my mind.

I was so upset when Carlos closed the old Hideout, just like when we had to leave my old house and move to this building. It's hard to leave a place that means so much, that's filled with happy memories. But in the end, it's not the room that matters. We have the new Hideout now, but what makes it great isn't that it's bigger and can fit a couch. It's the people. It's Nora, and Elena, Oliver, and Miles. It's the fact that we can be together again.

And that's true for this apartment building, too. I still

miss our house, and our memories there, but what made it feel like home were my parents and sister. As I sit on this couch with them, knowing how much my parents care about me, and still care about each other—this is home.

That night, I head down to the basement for our game night. I can't wait to see my friends and hang out in our new space. I'm also excited because I came up with a new Hideout name. It's perfect, and I can't wait to share it with the others:

Home Base.

Because that's what the room is now. And it's what the five of us will be for each other. Home base.

Acknowledgments

First and foremost, this book wouldn't have gotten to this point without my brilliant editor, Mabel Hsu. Mabel, thank you for all of your brainstorming help and editorial guidance. I'm so proud of this story, and hope we get to work on many more together!

Being part of HarperCollins Katherine Tegen Books is a dream. To Katherine Tegen, Tanu Srivastava, Sam Benson, Laura Harshberger, Mark Rifkin, Erin Wallace, Kristen Eckhardt, Vaishali Nayak, Laura Mock, Amy Ryan, Megan Gendell, Patty Rosati, Mimi Rankin, and Katie Dutton: Thank you for all of your hard work and support.

To Ronique Ellis, huge thanks for my stunning cover

illustration! You captured Joy and the Hideout so beautifully.

To Alex Slater, thanks for being an amazing agent that I can always count on. I'm also grateful for the support of the entire Trident Media Group team.

Under normal conditions, writing a second book for publication is a challenge. It was tough to juggle drafting this book and publicizing From the Desk of Zoe Washington. Looking back, that was the easy part, because then I had to edit it during a global pandemic! I honestly couldn't have completed the work without my incredible husband, Steve, who made sure I had the space and time to get it done while stuck at home. Thank you for always believing in me.

To Lorien Lawrence, thank you for being my first reader and keeping me accountable while I wrote this book! And to Shannon Doleski and Tanya Guerrero, whose cheerleading helped me get to the other side.

It means the world to have my parents, family, and friends champion my books. I want to give a special shout out to my bestie Jenifer Parker. Thanks for being excited for every single milestone I reach, no matter how big or small. You're the best hype woman and I love you!

To the community of librarians, educators, and booksellers who champion my stories and help them find readers: I'm grateful for all that you do, especially during hard times.

Finally, to all my young readers: Thank you for reading Zoe's and Joy's stories, and for all of your enthusiasm. You make this job so much fun. Keep reading and dreaming!